J.T. EDSON'S
FLOATING OUTFIT

The toughest bunch of Rebels that ever lost a war, they fought for the South, and then for Texas, as the legendary Floating Outfit of "Ole Devil" Hardin's O.D. Connected ranch.

MARK COUNTER was the best-dressed man in the West: always dressed fit-to-kill. **THE YSABEL KID** was Comanche fast and Texas tough. And the most famous of them all was **DUSTY FOG**, the ex-cavalryman known as the Rio Hondo Gun Wizard.

J.T. Edson has captured all the excitement and adventure of the raw frontier in this magnificent Western series. Turn the page for a complete list of Berkley Floating Outfit titles.

J. T. EDSON'S
FLOATING OUTFIT
WESTERN ADVENTURES
FROM BERKLEY

J.T. Edson

OLD MOCCASINS
ON THE TRAIL

860594

BERKLEY BOOKS, NEW YORK

Originally printed in Great Britain

This Berkley book contains the complete
text of the original edition.
It has been completely reset in a typeface
designed for easy reading, and was printed
from new film.

OLD MOCCASINS ON THE TRAIL

A Berkley Book/published by arrangement with
Transworld Publishers Ltd.

PRINTING HISTORY
Corgi edition published 1981
Berkley edition/November 1985

ISBN: 0-425-08278-4

A BERKLEY BOOK® TM 757,375
Berkley Books are published by The Berkley Publishing Group,
200 Madison Avenue, New York, New York 10016.
The name "BERKLEY" and the stylized "B"
with design are trademarks belonging to
Berkley Publishing Corporation.
PRINTED IN THE UNITED STATES OF AMERICA

For Joy from Turner's and Hazel the Income Tax,
a vodka and lime and a port and lemon,
if I remember correctly.

AUTHOR'S NOTE

Although one version of the events recorded herein appeared as Part Three, the Ysabel Kid in "Sam Ysabel's Son," THE TEXAN, *we did not at that time have access to the full details. These have now been made available to us by Alvin Dustine "Cap" Fog, along with permission to reproduce them.*

We realize that, in our present "permissive" society, we could include the actual profanities used by various people who appear in this volume, but we do not concede that a spurious desire to produce "realism" is a valid reason for doing so.

As we do not conform with the current "trendy" pandering to the exponents of the metric system, with the exception of calibers appropriate to various weapons—e.g., Luger 9mm—we will continue to employ miles, yards, feet, inches, pounds and ounces when referring to measurements and weights.

Lastly, to save our "old hands" from repetition and for the benefit of new readers, we are giving details of the background and special qualifications of the Ysabel Kid in an appendix.

J.T. EDSON,
Active member, Western Writers of America
Melton Mowbray,
Leics.,
England.

CHAPTER ONE

You Didn't Learn Well Enough

Although that exceptionally fine type of sporting fish would not become present in any numbers until "farm" breeding and stocking was developed as a means of catering to the needs of an ever growing volume of anglers, the Rio Grande, being borne of snow-fed brooks, resembles a typical trout stream near its source in the mountains of southwestern Colorado. Hurtling along a rocky course through high country forests of spruce, fir and aspen, it descends some five thousand feet by the time it has covered about eighty miles. The slope becomes less severe and its flow more serene on reaching the park-like San Luis Valley. At the period in which this narrative is set there were many ranches in the region and farmers were also obtaining a footing, but drawing water from the river and from deep wells for irrigation or other purposes had not as yet started to take any discernible toll of the water level. The current was still far from being the weakling it would later become as a result of such depletions. Long a powerful and major force in molding the landscape, the waters on entering New Mexico, passed through the Rio Grande Gorge which had been carved by the current over the centuries more than a thousand feet into the solid rock.

Continuing due south, through the heart of New Mexico, the Rio Grande passes along the Valle Grande and White Rock Canyons, then skirts the sheer rocky walls where Fourteenth Century Indians built their cave homes. By now it is flowing through semidesert country and, having picked up several tributaries along the way, has gradually widened. Although many large trees grow near the banks, the general

1

terrain consists of spare growths of pinyon pines and junipers, mingled with a few prickly pear cacti. Below Albuquerque, a few larger tributaries start to make themselves felt as do many smaller streams which are dry much of the time. However, following the infrequent cloudbursts, these "dry washes" suddenly turn into seething and racing torrents. By the time their respective flows slow to a trickle and finally disappear, a great deal of additional water and a massive quantity of silt has been added to the river, the latter to the detriment of the various man-made lakes and reservoirs down stream.

Wending its way southeast to form the border between Texas and Mexico—it is known as the *"Rio Bravo"* by the latter country—the Rio Grande during the mid-1870's, despite being subject to seasonal variations to is flow, was still free from the hands of the dam builders, and impoundments like mighty Elephant Butte reservoir were not even envisaged. Nor was there, at that time, any need for the legal agreements between various States and Mexico, whereby the amount of river water each was allowed to abstract was established.

With its volume and grandeur enhanced by the joining of the Rio Conchos from the Mexican shore, the Rio Grande makes the enormous curve in which nestles the spectacular scenery and immense cattle ranches of the Big Bend country of Texas. So large an area is encompassed that, even to this day, the landscape within is almost unbelievably varied and, to a great extent, unspoiled by the hand of man. There are stretches of sandy lowlands, dense reed jungles and three narrow canyons each approaching fifteen hundred feet in depth. The cool evergreen forests of the Chisos Mountains gave way to such desert vegetation as *yuccas* and *mesquite* on the lower slopes. Yet a further change comes when the fertile bottomlands are reached. There, the river nestles in the shade of giant cottonwoods, willows and other large, water loving trees.

Below the Big Bend, the river is further swollen by major tributaries such as the Pecos and Devil's Rivers of Texas and the Rio Salado from Mexico, then the Rio Grande drifts onwards to the east until it forms the delta which is known locally as the "magic valley." There, until the early 1940's—when the pressures of a global war led to its "development"—the terrain was covered by a thorny forest of *mesquite,* various types of cactus and a host of unusual trees found nowhere else in the United States.

Finally, having covered some eighteen hundred miles from its small beginnings in the mountains of Colorado, its meanderings end in the Gulf of Mexico.

In the days before "civilization" spread its inevitable way over most of the area across which the Rio Grande flowed, wild life abounded throughout its length. Mountain lions, bobcats, jaquarundi, occasionally jaguar or ocelot strayed north from deeper in Mexico. Black bear, less frequently the Texas subspecies of flathead grizzly and numerous smaller four legged predators preyed upon the herbivores. Depending upon the region and nature of the terrain, these could be whitetail or mule deer, raccoon, ringtailed coatamundi—although the last two were omnivorous by choice—pronghorn antelope, Rocky Mountain or Mexican bighorn sheep, the pig-like Texas collared peccary—known locally as the *"javelina"*—jackrabbits, armadilloes and small rodents too numerous to be listed individually.

Another source of sustenance for the predators, which frequently brought them into conflict with the human population and caused them to be hunted close to extinction as time went by, were free ranging horses and longhorn cattle. Half wild and only semidomesticated at best although their kind had played a major part in helping the people of Texas to regain financial stability following their support of the Confederate cause in the War Between The States,[1] the latter were formidable adversaries to the predators and well able to take care of themselves while living in close to natural conditions.

Among the birds, flocks of wild turkey could be found where the terrain suited their specialized needs as—in the appropriate seasons—could the sandhill and large whooping crane. With the exception of the far from frequent appear-

---

1. *How this came about is recorded in:* GOODNIGHT'S DREAM, FROM HIDE AND HORN *and* SET TEXAS BACK ON HER FEET. *J. T. E.*

ance of a bald or golden eagle, all three species were generally safe from the depredations of the winged eaters of flesh. Nevertheless, various types of hawks, falcons and owls found sustenance in plenty by preying upon the vast variety of smaller birds, animals, reptiles and amphibians. Nor did the scavengers such as the black, or turkey buzzard ever go hungry for any extended period under such beautiful conditions.

The species *Salmo* and *Salvelinus* might be poorly represented in the waters of the Rio Grande, but otherwise the fish population was diverse and far from inconsiderate, if short of those regarded as "game" or "sporting" by human anglers. Where conditions were suitable, rock, warmouth, white, yellow and—most highly prized by fishermen— largemouth bass could be found. There were green, redear, longear, yellowbreast and spotted sunfish. Strangely, however, the generally widespread and prolific white and yellow perch were absent. In the slower stretches, yellow, brown and black bullheads[2] grubbed contentedly in the muddy bottom oblivious of the silt. Neither the northern nor the mighty mukellunge pike were present, but their smaller relative, the pickerel, helped keep the fish population in check. Although they did not attain the sizes of their kin in the Mississippi or those close to the hide and tallow factories on the Brazos River,[3] the blue and yellow catfish could be found as—in swifter and cleaner water than was favored by the others—could the channel catfish.[4] If sought in the lower reaches, the bowfin and freshwater drum might be caught.

---

2. *The black bullhead,* Ictalurus melas, *is frequently sold by aquarist suppliers as a "coldwater catfish" for scavenging in goldfish tanks. Their release into certain rivers in Europe has allowed them to multiply to plague proportions. J. T. E.*

3. *An example of the sizes to which the blue,* Ictalurus furcatus, *and yellow or flat-head catfish,* Pylodictis olivaris, *could attain under suitable conditions is given in:* THE HIDE AND TALLOW MEN. *J. T. E.*

4. *A description of one method of fishing for channel catfish,* Ictalurus punctatus, *can be found in:* SET AFOOT. *J. T. E.*

Towards the mouth, where the junction with the Gulf of Mexico turned the water blackish, tarpon and some other generally sea dwelling species cruised. Throughout the length of the river, there were also a multitude of smaller varieties known to anglers as "bait fish" and upon which larger types, as well as some birds and animals fed.

Among the predators which sought food from among the fishes of the Rio Grande were the goosander, red breasted and hooded mersanger. Nor were these the only members of the duck family (although the tastes of the others were generally more vegetarian) to find the river attractive along a considerable proportion of its length. It provided an area most congenial for a halt for a meal while flying south to winter in Mexico, Central and—in a few cases—the northern portion of South America, or when returning to their respective breeding grounds in Canada and Alaska.

Many transient species of the family, *Anatidae* could be found along the Rio Grande when the season and weather conditions were right. Greenwinged and blue winged teal, bufflehead, greater and lesser scaup, gadwall, shoveler, pintail, mallard—ancestors of the domesticated farmyard duck—redhead, canvasback, ruddy and black duck each found a temporary habitat most suited to its needs and where there was little or no competition for food amongst the various species.

Of the sub-family, *Anserinae*, only the majestic trumpeter swan could be regarded as a genuinely wild visitor. What few groups of mute swams existed resulted from birds which had escaped semi-captivity after having been brought to the United States from Europe. Slightly smaller than the swans, but more highly regarded as a sporting proposition, the Canada goose also found the Rio Grande a worthwhile stopping place when making its annual migratory flights. While their size served to preclude them from forming a regular item on the menu of most animal, avian or piscatorial predator, human hunters had long sought this latter species out.

Having been fortunate enough to avoid the perils of the long flight south from their summer breeding grounds in the marshes of Canada, then successfully passed the winter months feeding in a part of Mexico only rarely visited by man, the coming of warmer weather had once again started the species, *Branta canadensis,* moving to the north. After flying for a long distance at the point of the habitual V-shaped wedge of one skein, attaining a speed of between fifty and sixty miles per hour on occasion, the older gander led its followers back to earth on a suitable section of the Rio Grande.

And, by doing so, inadvertently played a part in the events which followed!

Whether seen while grazing on land, or—as the flock were at that moment—swimming, fully grown Canada geese present a most striking appearance. Unlike many kinds of birds, the pheasant being a good example, there was little or no sexual dimorphism to indicate which was male and which female. Both sexes are light gray on the breast, tapering to a white along the underbelly and to the tail. The back and wing coverings are a darker gray. Every bird has an unusually long neck for its size, which changes coloration at the body line to become a pure black. This extends all over the head, with the exception of a large vertical white patch descending from near the crown and all the way down the face. When fully grown and in the peak of condition, the birds weigh between eight and ten pounds for a body length of up to thirty-six inches and a wingspan which could spread to a good six feet in width.

Although Canada geese as a species were extremely wary, such wisdom was only acquired with the passing of time. Having a life span equaling that of a human being, the older the bird, the greater grew its experience and alertness.

Leading its skein northwards, the oldest gander had selected the area in which it brought them to rest with the skill developed over the years of taking similar flights. It took account of how to make the most of changing weather conditions. It had chosen a spot where the river spread out beyond a gentle bend to form a large pool. Out in the center, there was an all round vision that would render the task of a stalking predator almost impossible to accomplish without detection. There was a sizeable sandbar extending from each shore, but neither offered any cover. Furthermore, although surrounding terrain was hilly and covered by woodland, the trees and undergrowth ended too far from the edge of the water to allow any creature to approach unseen.

Yet, in spite of the precautions, a predator was managing to stalk the birds without putting them to flight!

Several times since shortly after the geese had descended, wild melons had floated downstream. However, having seen similar objects behaving in such a fashion on numerous occasion with no danger to itself, the oldest gander did not raise the alarm and lead the skein into the safety of the air. Instead, it had done no more than swim a short distance away and allow the dislodged fruit to pass. With one exception, the rest of the big birds had followed the example of their leader.

The exception, a gander which was just attaining full growth and approaching the age when he would seek independence from his experienced elders, paid no attention to the latest of the floating greenish-yellow spheres to put in an appearance. It did not seem to present any great cause for concern. It was drifting along in a manner little different from that of its predecessors.

But there was a *major* difference!

The only outwards divergence in the appearance of the melon was a pair of small holes bored through the skin. If the young gander had employed its exceptionally keen vision to the best advantage, it might have noticed a pair of eyes a curious red-hazel in color watching its every movement from behind the apertures. It could also have discerned, if it had been more wary and observant, that the latest apparently inanimate and harmless object was not merely being carried along by the river.

The latest melon was, in fact, moving in a way which indicated it was not entirely dependent upon the flow of the current!

Because of its lack of the kind of caution required to ensure a lengthy life in a world filled with potential enemies, the young gander was presenting an opportunity to the secret predator responsible for the melon's peculiar behavior.

The predator which had found a means of circumventing the generally effective protective precautions of the Canada geese was a human being!

On his way to visit a friend of long standing who was in business as saddler in the small border town of Wet Slim, the Ysabel Kid's attention had been attracted by the *"eaur-awk, eaur-awk"* call of the wild geese while they were still almost a mile beyond the southern shore of the Rio Grande. Watching them as they approached, he had identified their species and was pleased by the sight of them dropping towards the river. Knowing old Jock McKie had a liking for such meat and possessed great skill in adding to its flavor during cooking, he had decided to try and obtain one of the birds as a present.

Thinking back to the lessons of his childhood and later experiences,[5] the Kid had realized that the task which he proposed undertaking would be anything except a sinecure!

The summation had proved to be correct!

Employing the encyclopedic knowledge of much of the Rio Grande between El Paso and the Gulf of Mexico, which he had acquired during his far from peaceful formative years, the Kid had appreciated that the pool selected by the oldest gander as a resting place would not lend itself to any easy means of supplying his friend with the main ingredient for a meal. Excellent shot through he undoubtedly was, and aided by the fact that he would be using a superlative "One Of A Thousand" Winchester Model of 1873 rifle—to which no weapon *in its class* was equal "much less superior" for accuracy[6]—he could not rely upon making a head shot from the closest distance he would be able to attain without frightening away such a wary quarry. What was more, should he strike the body of even the largest of the assembled birds, the .44 caliber bullet propelled by the force of forty grains of prime du Pont black powder detonating would mushroom

5. *Details of the career, special qualifications and armament of the Ysabel Kid are given in the Appendix to this volume. J. T. E.*
6. *How the Winchester Model of 1873 "One Of A Thousand" rifle came into the possession of the Ysabel Kid is told in: GUN WIZARD. J. T. E.*

on impact and cause so much destruction of the eating meat that he would be subject to cheerfully derisive comments from McKie.

Having considered the situation, the Kid had accepted that he must adopt a far less easy method to shooting if he was to acquire the present for the elderly saddler. With that point conceded, he had set about making preparations for the task. Finding a clearing a short distance upstream of the pool which offered all he needed, he had first removed the saddle and bridle from his magnificent white stallion. With this done, knowing the horse would remain in the vicinity although not tied in any way, he had divested himself of the majority of his attire. Leaving this with the remainder of his property, except for the one piece of his armament he would require, he had set about arranging a diversion which he had hoped would permit him to reach his quarry undetected. Collecting some of the wild melons from a patch in the clearing, he had launched all except one in the direction of the bend which was concealing him from the geese. Employing no other tool than the razor sharp, needle pointed blade of his massive James Black bowie knife, he had hollowed out the exception and punctured two eye-holes in the skin. Placing the remains over his head and holding them in position with his left hand, he had waded into the river. On reaching a depth sufficient to permit him to float in a vertical posture, he had allowed himself to be carried by the current after the other fruit he had launched.

In spite of it having been several years since he had last performed the technique, the Kid had retained the skills acquired in his childhood. Having come into sight of his quarry and avoided arousing suspicion by allowing himself and his camouflage to behave in the same fashion as the unprepared melons, he had studied them. Choosing the bird which he considered was most suitable for his needs, he had made his selection by comparing its size with the other members of the skein. Satisfied by its incautious behavior that it was a young male, he considered it would still be sufficiently tender fleshed to provide the best possible meal. With the decision reached, he had started to maneuver himself and the hollow melon in the appropriate direction.

Watching with satisfaction as the distance between himself and the young gander decreased and there was no trace of it becoming suspicious, the Kid concluded it was now close enough for him to achieve his purpose. Sucking in a deep breath, to ensure his lungs were filled with air, he removed his left hand and lowered his head from its covering. Having done so, grasping the bowie knife in his right fist, he thrust himself forward beneath the water. Guided by instinct rather than vision, his left hand thrust out to grasp the unsuspecting gander by the right leg.

Even as the big bird let out a startled squawk which sent the rest of the skein into the air, the thrashing of its wings notwithstanding, it was dragged beneath the surface of the pool. Coming around, just as much in response to subconscious guidance as the grab with the other hand had been, the weapon in the Kid's right fist found its intended mark. Biting into the throat of the struggling gander, the blade ripped so deeply it practically severed the head and a flood of released life blood gushed upwards. Already the spasdomic efforts of his victim were rendering it difficult for him to retain his hold on the leg. The increase in the violent motions caused by the response of the nervous system to the sudden close-to-decapitation, wrenched the limb from his fingers. But although the gander floated to the surface, there was no danger of it escaping.

Coming up a short distance from his lifeless, if still moving, victim, the Kid shook his head to clear the water from his eyes and cleansed his lungs by expelling the air they held with a snort. Using his free hand to thrust back hair as black as the wing of a deep South crow, he trod water while waiting for the motions of the gander to come to an end.

"They do say you live and learn," the successful hunter remarked, his voice a pleasant tenor and the accent that of a native-born Texan, as he began to swim towards his now unmoving victim. "Trouble being, you lived too short and you didn't learn well enough. Anyways, you won't be wasted more than your feathers, bones, beak and feet the way old

Jock McKie'll fix you for eating when I get you to him."

Towing the bird at the conclusion of his sentiment, the Kid struck out with his knife filled right hand towards the Texas shore. As the water shallowed, he came to his feet.

Six foot in height, the body of the successful hunter was naked except for the blue breech-clout traditionally worn by a Comanche warrior. His body was scarred as a result of knife and gun shot wounds, but powered by wiry muscles indicative of an almost tireless strength. Indian dark like the rest of his skin, his face was handsome and that of a young man. Apart from his red-hazel eyes, which spoiled an impression that was deceptive, his features had an almost babyish innocence. Wading on to dry land, his movements were those of one who possessed great agility and would be capable of acting very swiftly.

Grinning in satisfaction, the Kid swung the lifeless body of the gander across his left shoulder. Allowing the bowie knife to dangle by his right side, he strolled leisurely away from the edge of the pool and towards the place at which he had left his horse and property.

CHAPTER TWO

Kill the Bastard!

"Hold it up and take a look *there!*" Sebastian Montalban ejaculated in his native Spanish, reining his blaze-faced bay gelding to a halt and pointing ahead. "This is our *lucky* day, *amigos!*"

"It sure is, "Tian!" enthused Alfredo Acusar, also bringing his mount to a stop and gazing across the clearing at the objects which had provoked the comments from his companion.

"Whose are they, I wonder?" Tomas Acusar inquired, duplicating the actions of his elder brother and Montalban, and gazing around the deserted clearing in a puzzled manner.

"Who cares?" Alfredo countered. "He's not around as far as I can see."

"Could be he's taking a bath down at the river," Montalban supplemented, forming this conclusion from what he could see. "And, as he doesn't have any guns with him, I don't think he'll cause us any trouble."

In their early twenties, the trio of Mexicans were all tall and slim. They wore fairly expensive *charro* clothing—that of Montalban being of somewhat better quality than that of either of his companions—carelessly, as if the maintenance of the garments was of no importance. Nor was it, to their way of thinking. Being *bandidos* by choice and members of the most notoriously successful gang in Mexico, although their status among their associates was far from high—despite Montalban being a nephew of its leader—they never felt the need to take care of their property.

None of the trio had heard the phrase, or would have

12

understood it if they had, but their "philosophy" was simple. To their way of thinking, they could always obtain a replacement for anything ruined as a result of neglect by employing the same type of illegal means by which the original had been acquired. Few storekeepers in north eastern Mexico would dare deny anything a member of Ramon Peraro's band demanded. Those who did quickly came to regret the decision and, provided they survived the penalty, were invariable more obliging in the future.

There was, it must be admitted, an exception to the rule where the care of the property owned by the trio was concerned. Reckless and irresponsible though they tended to be where clothing, jewelry, saddlery and mounts were concerned, they had sufficient common sense to pay reasonable attention to the condition of their weapons. The Colt Peacemaker in the fast draw holster and the fighting knife which swung from every belt were all kept in a state of serviceability.

Being engaged upon what had so far proved an unproductive raiding expedition north of the Rio Grande, which they as Mexicans referred to as the *Rio Bravo,* the three young men were making their way towards the town of Wet Slim in the hope of finding some kind of loot to take back to Escopeta as evidence of their abilities. None of them had expected there would be any chance of acquiring booty in the unpopulated area of woodland through which they were passing and they were delighted by the discovery they had just made.

Although there was no sign of the owner, nor any clue as to how the objects in the clearing had come there, the several items all had a monetary value and would be worth collecting.

There were also, if the trio had been given to perception, indications of who owned the property which was arousing their interest and avarice!

Lying on its side, the owner clearly being a careful man and aware of the damage which might occur if it was set down on its skirts, was a low horned, double girthed saddle with a plain bridle, bit and reins across its seat. A coiled lariat was attached to the horn, but the bulky bedroll—still wrapped in a waterproof tarp—had been unstrapped from the cantle and placed close by the rig. On the bedroll was a low crowned, wide brimmed J.B. Stetson hat—its shape, like the style of the saddle, suggesting the absent owner was a Texan—a bandana which was still tightly rolled, a shirt and a pair of trousers. As a clue to the assumption made by Montalban with regards to his absence, the owner had left behind his boots—a grey woollen sock hanging from each one—but there was no sign of any kind of underclothing. Like the saddle, with the exception of the socks, every item of attire was black.

This alone should have offered the *bandidos*, young and inexperienced though they might be, a suggestion as to the identity of the man who had left the property in the clearing!

An even stronger pointer was available!

Sharing the seat of the saddle with the means of guiding the horse lay a black leather gunbelt. In the low cavalry twist draw holster on its right side, the butt pointing forward when worn, was an old walnut handled Colt Model of 1848 Dragoon revolver. Although the sheath at the left was empty, its massive dimensions were a clear indication of the type of knife for which it was intended. Even more evidential of ownership, particularly if a closer examination was made, was the rifle in the boot on the uppermost left side of the rig. While the "furniture" of the standard factory issue of the Winchester Model of 1873 was brown, the exposed butt of this specimen had been made from top quality black walnut and carried an inset silver plate with writing inscribed thereon.

Perception had never been the strong point of Montalban, or of either of the Acusar brothers. In spite of all the indications which would have warned a person of greater discernment of a possible and very grave danger to them if any interference was made with the items in the clearing, they ignored the signs and thought only of their improved fortune. Since becoming involved in the activities of the gang, the brothers had frequently been the objects of derision from the older and more experienced members. Nor, for all his relationshp to their leader, had Montalban found himself precluded from receiving similar treatment. Therefore, they were thinking only of taking the booty which chance had thrown their way to be displayed in *Bernado's Cantina* at Escopeta. The only consideration they gave to the owner of the property was whether it would be worth the effort to find and kill him, or if it might make a more amusing tale to announce they had subjected him to the humiliation of continuing his journey clad only in whatever undergarments he happened to be wearing.

"Hell, if he's *loco* enough to leave his gear lying around like this, he deserves to have to walk wherever he's going in his union suit or buff naked," Montalban scoffed, in answer to the point having been raised by the younger of the brothers. Swinging from his saddle and allowing the reins to dangle free, "ground hitching" the bay, he continued impatiently, "Come on. Let's go get it!"

Dismounting, Alfredo and Tomas Acusar left their equally well trained mounts in the same fashion. As they set off across the clearing, they made no attempt to go ahead of their companion. A sense of politeness was not responsible for them allowing him to precede them. He was the nephew of their leader and, as such, they reluctantly conceded the claim each knew would be forthcoming that he was granted the first pick at the loot. However, as he was dependant upon them for companionship and support, they felt sure he would not be excessive in his appropriations.

"Madre de dios!" Alfredo ejaculated, staring harder as the realization came that the subject of his exclamation was no ordinary run-of-the-mill Winchester. "Just look at that *rifle!*"

"I told you boys this is *my* lucky day!" Montalban replied, having arrived at an identical conclusion and intending to establish his prior claim to the magnificent weapon. "And it is!"

Normally, the assumption to the right of picking first would have been allowed to pass unchallenged!

However, on this occasion, the piece of loot was far more valuable than anything else which had come the way of the trio!

"Then why not see just how good your *luck* is?" Alfredo suggested, raising his avaricious gaze from the magnificent rifle.

"How do you mean?" Montalban demanded rather than asked, also turning his attention from the prize he considered to be rightfully his, and looking at the older of the Acusar brothers with suspicion and menace.

"It's plain enough," Alfredo answered, showing no sign of being put out or scared by the obvious challenge directed his way. "You reckon you're so lucky, so let's spin a coin to see who gets the rifle."

"Why should we?" Montalban snarled.

"Because *I* want it that way!" Alfredo declared uncompromisingly.

"Is that *so?*" Montalban spat out, lifting his right hand until it was hovering above the butt of his Colt Civilian Model Peacemaker.[1]

"That's the way I figure it's going to be!" Alfredo asserted, also adopting a position of threat and readiness. "And don't bother telling me Don Ramon is your uncle. I *know* he is and I also know he *always* says the loot is shared out fairly."

"Hey!" Thomas put in, watching his sibling and their companion growing more angry and preparing to act in the capacity of peacemaker. Before he could go any further, a movement caught the corner of his eye and, looking around, he pointed saying, "Look *there!*"

Following the advice they had been given, the two young *bandidos* gazed across the clearing. What they saw temporarily drove all thoughts of hostility from each of them. They had closed their hands about the butts of their weapons, but neither drew it from its holster. Instead, they stared at a magnificent white stallion which was approaching through the trees from the direction of the river. It was the kind of horse each had dreamed of owning. While there was a glint

---

1. *Information regarding the different types of Colt Model "P" of 1873, commonly known as the "Peacemaker", can be found in those volumes of the* Floating Outfit *series which follow* THE PEACEMAKERS *in the chronological sequence. J. T. E.*

of metal on its hooves indicating it had recently been shod, it conveyed an aura of being as wild and free as any *manadero* master of a band of mustangs.

"*Madre de dios!*" Montalban ejaculated. "What a *beauty!*"

"I suppose *you're* going to say *that's* yours as well?" Alfred inquired coldly, swinging his attention from the stallion as he detected the note which had entered Montalban's voice.

"And what if I am?" Montalban wanted to know, once again bristling aggression as he concluded that he must quell the revolt against his authority or he would never again be able to exert it over at least the elder brother.

Being less involved in the dispute over the division of the loot than his sibling or their self appointed leader, as he accepted that he would as usual, be compelled to take whatever was left, Tomas was growing aware of something which was still escaping the attention of the other two. The remembrance which was starting to take form was of something far from pleasant or likely to create a sense of peace of mind. He was considering what could be implied by the combination of clothing which was all black, the archaic type of revolver butt forward in the holster, the suggestion of the type of knife carried in the empty sheath, the extra special Winchester and the magnificent white stallion.

Such attire, armament and horse was owned by a man who, while far from old in actual years, was already a legend on both sides of the *Rio Bravo!*

A man who would be guaranteed to have the strongest objections against anybody who tried to make off with his property!

One who, furthermore, was said to be a sufficiently competent and savage fighter to render any attempt to steal from him hazardous in the extreme!

While Thomas could not imagine why such a man as *el Cabrito* would leave the valuable property untended, he felt that a warning of his suppositions was *most* advisable!

"Alfredo, Sebastian!" the younger brother gasped. "Do you know—?"

"Suppose I say I want that horse and the rifle?" Montalban asked, ignoring the words.

"Then you're going to have to go through *me* to get them!" Alfredo asserted, paying just as little attention to his brother.

"So that's the way of it?" Montalban hissed.

"That's the way of it!" Alfredo confirmed.

"Hey!" Tomas yelped. "This gear belongs to—!"

"All right," Montalban said, relaxing a trifle as he realized he was outnumbered by the brothers and recollecting that the younger had always been ready to support the elder. "I'll take the rifle, you have the horse. Go and get it. But watch out, it looks meaner than hell!"

"I'll watch it, don't worry," Alfredo declared, deducing what had caused their companion to change his mind. "And, if *it* tried anything, I'll kill the bastard!"

"Alfredo!" Tomas almost wailed, watching his sibling start to walk across the clearing. "This gear belongs to—!"

"*Us!*" the elder brother interrupted, without halting or looking back. "Just keep watch to make sure it stays that way!"

"It belongs to *el Ca*—!" Tomas shouted, but once more was not allowed to divulge the information.

In fact, his attempt produced a reaction its maker had not anticipated!

From all appearances, the threat made by the older of the Acusar brothers might need to be carried out as a result of the well intentioned behavior of his sibling!

Halting on the edge of the clearing on hearing the shouted words, having been to the river to slake its thirst, the stallion tossed its head and let out a snort charged with menace. Like most of its species, it was possessed of better hearing and sense of smell than vision. Therefore, while it had been able to see the three male figures in the clearing as it approached through the woodland, it was not able to make out who they were due to there having been no assistance from the breeze. All it had known until Tomas yelled was that there were intruders encroaching upon an area in which it and the property of its master had been left. The sound and timbre of the voice removed any possibility of them being friendly.

The response elicited by the discovery struck the three young Mexicans as familiar. It was similar to that of a *manadero* seeing a strange stallion in the vicinity of its harem of mares. Nor did any of them consider the evidence of its domestication would make the big white horse any the less dangerous than a *manadero*.

"You'd better get ready to shoot it, *amigo!*" Montalban warned, seeing a way in which he might ensure ownership of the rifle and, if fortunate, the horse. Starting to take out and cock his Colt, he went on so as to prevent the younger brother drawing the wrong—or, from his own point of view, *right*—conclusion with regards to his motives, "Tomas and I'll cover you in case you don't drop him first shot!"

Never the quickest of thinkers and, despite having known their companion for long enough to have been made suspicious by such uncharacteristic behavior, the younger Acusar also reached for his holstered Colt. He responded without thinking, or offering to continue his warning with regards to his deductions regarding the owner of the property. The way in which the large white stallion was acting drove every other thought from his head.

Until—!

Some instinct, rather than having heard any sounds, caused Tomas to glance over his shoulder. What he saw drove every other consideration away immediately. Yet, although he did not realize it, the sight was proof that he had been correct in his assumptions.

Naked except for a blue breechclout and armed with a knife of proportions rendered, it seemed, even more enormous by his savage demeanor, the figure racing from the woodland behind the two young Mexicans had the appearance of a Comanche Dog Soldier coming to make an attack apart from his black hair being short instead of hanging at shoulder length.

Returning from his successful stalking and killing of the Canada goose, the Ysabel Kid had seen the trio as they were dismounting in the clearing. While he did not know *who* they were, their appearance had left him with no doubts over *what* they were. He was too far away at the first sighting to hear what was being said, but could guess what the subject under discussion would be. Furthermore, the years he had spent riding the border trails with his father as smugglers had done nothing to lead him to assume they would be dissuaded from their intentions by verbal means if, as he knew was almost certain to be the case, they were planning to steal the property he had left behind.

Guessing by the lack of response that his big white stallion had gone to drink from the river, at the point where he had entered to be carried around the bend and to his quarry, the Kid had prepared to defend his belongings. Armed only with his massive James Black bowie knife, effective a weapon though it might be in some circumstances, he was too well versed in such matters to want his presence to be discovered by the Mexican *bandidos*. Young and inexperienced as they clearly were, each was wearing a handgun which offered a greater range than his knife. With that point in mind, dropping his trophy, he had continued his advance as swiftly as stealth and caution would permit.

Just before the Kid had reached the edge of the clearing, he had seen his stallion returning. Despite being grateful for the distraction its arrival had caused, listening to the comments this elicited, he had been aware of the danger to the animal. He knew, even before he had seen it, what the response of discovering the strangers near his property would be. Hearing the remarks passed between the two older members of the party had confirmed his belief.

Moving forward, the Kid began to act as his upbringing as a *Pehnane* Comanche warrior dictated. Crossing the intervening space at a swift run, he had no intention of allowing the men to realize he was there any sooner than was absolutely necessary. To do so under a misguided sense of sporting behavior would be the height of folly which was against the nature of the *Nemenuh* brave-heart he had become. Nor was his decision produced solely by the Indian side of his birthright. As a white man, he was equally aware that there were few people around more ruthless and cold blooded than the average Mexican *bandido*. Even three so young would not have the slightest compunction over killing him without a chance if granted an opportunity. They would possibly be more violent because of their youth and a desire to prove themselves the equal of their older and more experienced *companeros*. In fact, they would prefer to make his death as painful and lingering as possible.

Watching the younger of the pair he was approaching start to look around, the Indian dark Texan let out the blood chilling war whoop of a Comanche warrior. He did not allow the effect of the yell alone to achieve his purpose. Even as it was bursting from him, he bounded into the air. As he was rising, he turned his lean and steel muscled body until it was almost parallel to the ground. He crashed into the backs of Tomas and Montalban, arriving an instant before the latter could deliver any warning of his coming. Both his victims were knocked in spinning sprawls out of his way, but they were not his main concern at that moment.

Already the big horse was displaying signs of aggression!

While the Kid was well aware of how effectively the stallion could protect itself, he was equally cognizant of the disadvantage it was under at that moment. The third Mexican was drawing his gun and there was enough space between them for him to be able to open fire before it could reach him no matter how fast it charged. Not, with so large a target, was he likely to miss and he would at the very least inflict a wound which might prove fatal. Therefore he had to be stopped.

Going to the ground in a rolling plunge after having knocked the other two *bandidos* out of his way, the Kid came to his knees at the end of it. Up and down whipped his right arm, the writhing of its muscles testifying to the force it was imparting. Leaving his hand, the great knife flew through the air. It was propelled by an owner who had attained the Comanche "man-name", *"Cuchilo"*—Spanish for "Knife"—while still a boy.

Hearing the commotion behind him, Alfredo Acusar took his attention from the white stallion for a moment. Starting to look around, his action was instinctive. It did nothing to save him. Traveling far too swiftly for him to be able to avoid it, the clip point of the great knife caught him on the temple. Made from almost the finest steel James Black was able to manufacture and given a perfect balance for throwing,[2] the velocity with which it arrived allowed the blade to pierce the bone. Head split open as if struck by an axe and killed instantly, the Mexican went down with the Colt flying harmlessly from his lifeless hand.

For all the success of the throw, it seemed the Kid had committed a grievous error of tactics.

By sending the knife to save his horse, the Texan had left himself with empty hands and he was not wearing any other weapon!

---

2. *Information about the composition of the finest type of steel James Black could manufacture is given in:* THE QUEST FOR BOWIE'S BLADE. *J. T. E.*

CHAPTER THREE

This Could Lose Me the Bet

The Ysabel Kid did not wait to watch the result of the throw!

Having dispatched the knife with what his instincts in such matters suggested was a sufficiently accurate aim to ensure a hit, the Indian dark Texan wasted not a moment before setting about arming himself again!

A glance around as he was rising informed the Kid he must do so with all the speed he could muster if he was to stay alive!

While he had sent both of the remaining Mexicans staggering as he burst between them, fortune had not favored him to any great extent. Only the younger of the pair had fallen. Not only had he retained his hold in his Colt Artillery Model Peacemaker, but it had cleared leather as he was going down. The other was still on his feet and was also still holding his revolver. It too was out and readily available to be used.

At such a moment, only an exceptional white man could have survived!

The Kid was responding not as a white man, but as a name warrior of the Comanche nation's *Pehnane* band; than which no better and more competent fighter existed!

Throwing himself forward, the Texan reached for the butt of his old Colt Model of 1848 Dragoon revolver. He had made the decision, knowing the handgun would be more easy to extract than trying to slide the Winchester Model of 1873 rifle from its boot. Under the circumstances which were prevailing, every split second counted and could make the difference between life and death. Grasping the walnut handle in his right fist as he was hurdling the saddle, he snatched the revolver from its holster in passing. With his left hand joining the right, as an aid to greater security and steadiness against the solid four pounds, one ounce weight, he swiveled around on landing. While doing so, he was drawing back the hammer with both thumbs and elevating the weapon to shoulder height at arms' length.

Catching his balance with an effort, Sebastian Montalban was momentarily too dazed to realize what was happening. By the time his wits had returned, he found he was in grave peril. The only thought elicited by the sight of Alfredo Acusar sprawling lifeless, the ivory hilt of a great knife rising above the bloody skull, was that the Indian dark figure was temporarily unarmed. However, he was taking very rapid steps to change that. Driven by a mixture of fear and anger, the young Mexican jerked up and fired his Colt Civilian Model Peacemaker.

Such a method was not conducive to accuracy!

Only very straight shooting could save Montalban!

Ignoring the lead from the gun of the Mexican as it hissed by his head, the Kid took aim along the eight inch long round barrel rather than using the notch on the tip of the hammer and the foresight. While the system would not have produced high scores in firing at a target on a range, it proved more than adequate for his current needs. In a vastly shorter time than the more formal way of sighting would have allowed, he was satisfied and squeezed the trigger. By removing his thumbs from the hammer, he allowed the mechanism to function and the Dragoon fired. Propelled along the rifling grooves, the .44 caliber round soft lead bullet left the muzzle followed by a cloud of white gas which briefly concealed his intended target. Flying with far greater accuracy than the one dispatched at him, it struck Montalban between the eyes and passed through to shatter its way out at the rear of the skull. Going over backwards, its recipient was dead before his body landed on the ground.

Sitting up and looking about him, Tomas Acusar let out a gobble which was closer to fear than fury. He saw his brother was down, and that the huge white stallion had halted its charge a few feet away and was moving restlessly, watching the motionless figure. Closer at hand, Montalban was being thrown from his feet by what was clearly a fatal wound. However, the response elicited by these sights was not provoked by grief and a desire to avenge their deaths. Self preservation alone caused Tomas to lift the Colt he was still holding and cut loose at the Indian-dark figure.

Thumb cocking the big Dragoon on its recoil, the Kid swung around at the waist. Once again, having a bullet narrowly miss him did nothing to detract from his purpose. As before, he relied upon aiming in a way more suited to a shotgun than a revolver and his weapon bellowed awesomely an instant after Tomas had tried to kill him. While the hit he made was much less serious than would otherwise have been the case (due to the rapidity with which it was discharged) it did all he required. Driven by the expanding gasses resulting from the explosion of fifty grains of prime du Pont black powder, ten more than was considered advisable for use in the cartridges of his *rifle*, the bullet merely ripped through the flesh at the point where the arm joined the shoulder. For all that, pain and shock pitched the young Mexican on to his back and he dropped his Peacemaker.

"Don't you even *try!*" the Kid warned, speaking the Spanish of the border country with the facility acquired by usage for much of his young life.

Swinging his head around as he was rolling on to his stomach and reaching towards the revolver, Thomas found himself staring into what seemed to be the muzzle of a heavy cannon such as he had once seen in an Army fort. Behind it, despite the words having been spoken so well in his native tongue that another Mexican might have uttered them, was a terrifying figure. The black hair might be short, but the features were those of a Comanche warrior on the warpath.

"D—Don't shoot!" Tomas howled, snatching his hand away from its objective as if he expected to find the butt red hot if he touched it. "I'm hit bad!"

"Go on now!" the Kid scoffed, lowering the hammer under the control of his thumbs and allowing the barrel of the Dragoon to sink out of alignment. "You're not more than scratched a mite!"

Watching and listening, Tomas became aware of a change coming over his assailant!

No longer was the voice savage and chilling. It now held an almost gentle, albeit sardonic, note. The difference, however, was only a little less disturbing because of this undertone. At the same time, the Indian dark features lost their bloodcurdling expression and took on a suggestion that was close to babyish innocence. This too was belied by the cold glint in the red hazel eyes which appeared to be boring into the head of the young Mexican and reading his innermost thoughts.

While the figure no longer resembled a Comanche braveheart on the hunt for coups and scalps, but was a white man, he was still clearly not one with whom it would be wise or safe to trifle.

"Y—!" Tomas gasped, sitting up and feeling gingerly at the wound to ascertain it was as trivial as his informant had suggested. Then, the words sounding more of a statement than a question, he continued, "You're *el Cabrito?*"

"Well, yes, I'll have to come right out and admit truthfully I'm *el Cabrito,*" the Texan confirmed, showing no offence at having his sobriquet corrupted by translating it into the name for a baby goat.[1] "And, seeing as we're getting down to it, who are you?"

"T—Tomas Acusar," the Mexican said, staring down at the reddened fingers of his hand which had carried out the exploration. "I'm bleeding bad, *Cabrito!*"

"Not nearly so bad's you'd've been should I have aimed to hit you anywhere more dangerous," the Kid pointed out, but he refrained from mentioning that pure chance alone had dictated the wound was so slight. "Your *amigos* weren't close to so lucky. Who are they?"

"The one by your horse is my brother, Alfredo," Tomas

---

1. *We have been informed recently that the current usage of the word,* cabrito, *is applied to a husband who is being made a cuckold by his wife. While this is the case now, we would point out the meaning of words change with the passing of time. We are old enough to remember when one could say a man was "gay" and merely mean that he was happy. J.T.E.*

replied, with no great display of grief or animosity. "And
the oth—!"

"And *who?*" prompted the Texan, the words having trailed
off as the speaker realized it might be very imprudent to
supply the information that the second victim was the nephew
of Don Ramon Peraro.

"I—I—!"

"Now you don't want for me to have to ask Blackie over
and have him see if he can do better than I did at hurting
you, do you?"

"Blac—?" Tomas commenced, knowing sufficient English to be aware of the meaning usually implied by the
word, then realized to what it was being applied on this
occasion. "No—No, *Cabrito!*"

With the appreciation, the Mexican turned his eyes to
the huge white stallion as it stood menacingly alongside the
body of his brother. He was not, however, giving any thought
to the example of a type of humor peculiar to the cowhands
of Texas which had created such a contradictory name.
Instead, he was remembering all the tales he had heard
regarding the savagery of the animal in question. At that
moment, despite previously having been inclined to dismiss
them as mere fabrications, he had no doubts about their
validity.

"Then you'd best tie me a brand on your *amigo* there
and *muy pronto,*" the Kid advised, as gently as the first
whisper of an arising Texas 'blue norther' storm and sounding just as potentially dangerous. "And who is he *kin* to?"

"Kin to?" Tomas repeated, startled at the perception suggested by the second part of the question.

"I'll give you some better than you deserve," the Texan
offered. "You tell me where you come from and I'll see if
I can figure it out for myself."

"Chihua—!" the Mexican began.

"Blackie" the Kid called over his shoulder.

"Escopeta!" Tomas revised hurriedly, deciding that to
continue the interrupted attempt at a bluff would produce
painful and possibly fatal repercussions.

"Escopeta, huh?" the Kid drawled pensively. "And he's

kin to Don Ramon Peraro?"

"Y—Yes," the young *bandido* replied, wondering if the admission would cost him his life which would be the most simple means of preventing the news of what had happened to Montalban reaching his *patron*.

"Are they *close* kin?" the Texan asked.

"N—Not all that close," Tomas admitted truthfully.

"Get up and toss away your knife," ordered the Kid.

"Wh—Why?" the Mexican inquired, with every evidence of alarm and fear.

"You don't reckon I'm trustful enough to starting fixing your wound while you're still wearing it, now do you?" the Kid queried sardonically. Then, looking from the body of Alfredo Acusar to the motionless shape of Montalban, he continued in English, "God damn it, this could lose me the bet!"[2]

"Ah, *Senora* and *Senorita* Castrillo," greeted Don Ramon Manuel José Peraro, striding across the barroom of *Bernardo's Cantina* with a proprietorial air which was valid as he and not the man whose name was painted on the wall above the main entrance was the owner of the establishment. Going to where two women followed by a third were coming downstairs from the second floor, he continued with genuine amiability, "The ransom money has arrived and, as I gave you my assurance would be the case, you are to be returned immediately to your family."

"*Immediately?*" asked the older of the two elegantly attired women, hopefully and yet clearly not entirely at ease, as she looked through the open front doors at the darkness outside the building.

"That was the assurance I gave to you and sent with the ransom note to your husband, *senora*," Peraro pointed out, halting so that the trio could complete the descent and stop before him on the floor of the barroom. "Your coach is ready and waiting with a driver and some of my most trusted

2. *Full details regarding "the bet"—this, incidentally, was the title under which we submitted the manuscript to our original publishers, Wagon Wheel Westerns, and was changed for reasons we were never told—are given in:* THE TEXAN. *J. T. E.*

men who will act as an escort until you are safely in the hands of the *vaqueros* that *Senor* Castrillo will have sent to the rendezvous. But, if you so wish, you may remain here until tomorrow morning."

"Here?" the woman repeated, looking about her with a mixture of revulsion and horror. "No. We'll go *now!"*

The decision would have struck most people as being understandable and wise!

Sitting at tables around the barroom, standing at its counter, or gathered in other places throughout the small Mexican town of Escopeta, were assembled as ruthless, bloodthirsty and murderous a bunch of criminals as could have been found in one spot anywhere in the world. There was no major or minor infraction of the law which had not been committed by at least one of them in his time. Nor was there any kind of outrage too evil and atrocious for somebody present to have carried out. Even the female occupants were far from fit company for any decent and respectable woman.

Only a man of exceptional courage and with powers of leadership and a great force of personality, backed by a complete disregard for the sanctity of human life, could control and command such a band of brutal ruffians.

Don Ramon Manuel José Peraro was such a man!

The fact that he was still alive and in good health was testimony to his capability and competence!

There was, in fact, no *bandido* surviving in Escopeta, who would consider opposing the will of their leader!

All those who had been sufficiently ill advised to do so in the past had met with sudden and painfully inflicted death within seconds of their incautious behavior becoming apparent!

Tall and slender, the *bandido* chief moved with an easy grace indicative of considerable power enhanced by the agility of a bull fighter, despite having attained forty years of strenuous life. Although the passage of time and a penchant for the good things in life had given a slight puffiness to his still handsome Latin features, at which one needed to look closely before discerning the real cruelty lurking beneath the veneer of charm, he was too wise to have allowed either time or indulgence to spoil his excellent physical condition to any noticeable degree. His attire was invariably that of an extremely wealthy *haciendero* and, when things were going well, he employed the manners and deportment of the kind of Old World Spanish *grandee* from which he claimed his stock had sprung. However, should things *not* be going well, his true nature came to the fore and everybody in his immediate vicinity knew it was time to step warily in his presence.

Courtly manners notwithstanding, Peraro was a very bad man to cross. It was a quality he needed to dominate the rapacious and cruel people who served as members of his band. The nickel plated Colt Civilian Model Peacemaker with its fancy silver Tiffany grips in the cross draw holster on the left side of his well polished black gunbelt and the ivory handled, finely chased ten inch long, spear pointed fighting knife sheathed at the right were far from being mere affectations intended to impress. When the situation demanded, he would use one or the other without the slightest hesitation and *very* effectively.

"The choice is entirely your own, my dear *senora*," the *bandido* chief claimed, his air magnanimous. "I trust you will apologize to your husband on my behalf for the deaths of your driver and guard and you will also see the wife of each receives the bag of money I'm sending them?"

"I will," *Senora* Castrillo promised before she could stop herself. Then, wondering what kind of man would make such a gesture after having shot down the driver of the coach before her eyes to emphasize his determination to have the ransom paid, she continued, "Can we go now, please?"

"As soon as you wish and with my assurance of your complete safety on the journey," Peraro declared, giving a bow as courtly as might have been made when *Cristóbal Colón* was granted permission and the means to set out upon the epic voyage which had resulted in the discovery of the "New World".[3] Looking past his ransomed captives briefly,

---

3. "Cristóbal Colón": *The Spanish name for Christopher Columbus, Italian-born navigator who discovered and claimed America for Spain on the 12th of October, 1492. J. T. E.*

he went on, "By the way, ladies, I trust you have both been treated with politeness, respect and consideration all the time you have been my guests?"

If any of the watching and listening crowd—which included some of the worst and most vicious villains to be found in Mexico—considered the Old World courtesy displayed by their leader a source of levity, they were too wise to allow their sentiments to become obvious. Even those who had the inclination remembered the fate of predecessors who had been sufficiently imprudent to let their derision or amusement show. As he took himself and his behavior very seriously, the recollection was not one which would encourage repetition.

"We ha—!" *Senora* Castrillo began.

"I *haven't* been!" asserted *Senorita* Castrillo heatedly, before her mother could finish, having drawn the correct deduction from the look which had accompanied the question. Turning and pointing at their escort, who was standing behind them at the foot of the stairs, she elaborated with an equal passion and annoyance, "This *person* has stolen my watch and the bracelet my fiancé gave me!"

Which was not, as any of the crowd in the barroom could have warned, the most politic way a pampered and well raised girl should lodge a complaint about the activities of Florencia Cazador!

The woman against whom the accusation was leveled had only just passed her twentieth birthday and, despite the fact that she should have held an exalted position in the society of the town, there was more than a suggestion of gypsy-like wildness about her. Shoulder long, straight black hair framed a beautiful olive brown face with the somewhat slanted eyes and Mongoloid features characteristic of many races of Indians in North America.[4] Five foot seven in height, she had a richly endowed, curvaceous and voluptuous figure

---

4. *How General Jackson Baines "Ole Devil" Hardin and his Japanese valet, Tommy Okasi, turned the similarity of facial characteristics to their advantage on an assignment during the Texas War of Independence is told in:* GET URREA. *J.T.E.*

which was emphasized rather than concealed by her attire.
Regardless of her personal desires, which would have selected elegant silken raiment and copious amounts of expensive jewelry—the largest and most ostentatious
available—she was not permitted to acquire such things.
For some reason known only to himself, having selected
her as his latest mistress, Peraro insisted she should remain
clad in little more than a simple multi-colored blouse, a
plain black skirt and that she should go barefoot after the
fashion of the maternal side of her bi-racial family.

"You lousy, 'mother-something' little liar!"[5] Florencia
yelled furiously and with what sounded like genuinely righ-
teous indignation, lunging at the girl behind outstretched
hands which reached talon-like for her hair.

The intended attack was not brought to fruition!

As the pair withdrew in alarm before her obvious anger,
Peraro stepped between his captives even more quickly than
his mistress and placed the palm of his left hand against her
face. Thrusting sharply, he sent her backwards until her feet
struck the bottom step and she sat with a thump on the
wooden stairs.

"Give them to me!" the *bandido* chief ordered, holding
forward his upturned and open right hand.

"I—I don't ha—!" Florencia began.

"Give them to me, damn you!" Peraro repeated savagely.

"I haven't got them with me!" the young woman answered sullenly.

"Then go and get them," Peraro thundered. "Now!"

Thrusting herself erect, Florencia fled up the stairs as
fast as her legs would carry her. Nothing was said by the
bandido chief or his victims while she was away. Silence
also fell all around the barroom as, knowing how he expected those who were taken for ransom to be treated while
awaiting the result of his demand for payment, the rest of
the men and women present interrupted their various activities in order to see what would happen. Returning just as
hurriedly, the young woman held out a small, jeweled gold

5. *See the second paragraph of our* AUTHOR'S NOTE. *J. T. E.*

watch of the kind which could be attached by a pin to the dress, and a wide bracelet made from the same precious material.

"H—Here they are, Ramon!" Florencia stated unnecessarily, thrusting the two items into the extended palm of the *bandido* chief. "I—I only took them as a joke!"

"Most amusing, but one of these days the lady you try to take them from might not just hand them over meekly," Peraro replied in a purring tone, accepting the watch and bracelet. "And *this* could happen!"

With the second part of his comment, the *bandido* chief swung his other arm to deliver a backhand slap to the face of his mistress which knocked her from her feet. Then, showing no greater concern than if he had swatted a bothersome fly, he returned the items to their owner.

"My apologies, ladies," Peraro went on, in a tone no different to that which had preceded the blow, bowing to each victim in turn. "No one who is a guest under my roof can be stolen from."

"So it seems," *Senora* Castrillo admitted, looking at Florencia with something close to pity. "May we go now?"

"Certainly," Peraro authorized. "I trust you will tell your husband and all his friends that you were treated properly while here. Please allow me to escort you to your coach."

CHAPTER FOUR

I Make an Example of the Captives

Getting to her feet slowly, Florencia Cazador felt with care at the cheek with had been struck by the *bandido* chief. After glancing at the blood which came from the corner of her mouth and was staining the back of her hand, she directed a glare at its cause. There was such concentrated hatred in the look that it was fortunate for her that he was walking away with the two ransomed captives and was unaware of her emotions. The expression came and went swiftly. She knew better than to offer any opportunity of being discredited in front of her rivals, any of whom would be pleased to take over the position of mistress to Don Ramon Manuel José Peraro. She composed her sullen beautiful features into an impassive mask and swung around to return upstairs where she could vent her anger in the privacy of her room.

"May I ask you a question, *senor?*" requested *Senora* Maria Castrillo, as she and her daughter were being escorted across the barroom of *Bernardo's Cantina* by the *bandido* chief.

"Of course, *senora,*" Peraro authorized politely.

"You killed our driver and guard, then kidnapped us," the woman said, being genuinely puzzled by the apparently contradictory character of the man who had held her and her daughter to ransom. "Yet, not only have you treated Teresa-Maria and myself with courtesy and consideration while holding us, and accommodated us far more comfortably than has been the case at many *posadas* in much larger towns than this, but you have taken nothing from our belongings and you punished that girl for stealing from us."

"Of course," the *bandido* chief answered, having had similar remarks made about his activities in the past.

"But *why* do you do it?" *Senora* Castrillo asked, looking through the open main entrance to where her coach was standing with its team hitched and a driver on the box. "Treat us in such a fashion, I mean. I always thought *bandi*—men like yourself—well, I thought they were less than gentle with those who fell into their hands."

"If you had fallen into the hands of *bandidos, senora,* and not a man like myself, your treatment probably would have been less than gentle, as you put it," Peraro replied. "But I pride myself on being a good businessman and one lesson every *businessman* learns and needs to remember if he is to be successful is that damaged goods lose their marketable value and do his reputation no good."

"I still don't understand," the woman claimed truthfully.

"Then allow me to explain," the *bandido* chief offered. "First, though, I trust you and your charming daughter will excuse me for referring to two such charming ladies as yourselves as 'goods'. You see, it is well known that *everybody* I kidnap is treated with kindness while waiting for the ransom money to be paid, and is returned promptly, with honor and all personal property intact, as soon as I receive the sum I have requested. Which, incidentally, is *never* excessive or beyond the means of the—customer, shall I say. Therefore, when I have a kidnapping carried out, the family of whoever I select knows there is nothing to fear—provided no attempt at a rescue is made and the money I ask for is forthcoming."

"What if a rescue is attempted?" queried the elder of the ransomed captives.

"That is *most* unfortunate for those who make the attempt, *senora,*" Peraro answered, in a matter of fact tone. "But even more *unfortunate* for the one who they are misguidedly *trying* to rescue. Need I say *more?*"

"No!" the woman said, barely able to restrain a shudder as the thought of what was implied by the second part of the explanation. Although she had never doubted that the money would be paid in the case of her daughter and herself, she could not prevent the next words being uttered. "And if the money *isn't* forthcoming?"

"As I said, *senora,*" the *bandido* chief replied, pleased with the way the conversation was going. It was one he always tried to have with departing captives and he usually sought a means to start such a talk if this was not forthcoming without his prompting. "I'm a *businessman* and to allow such a refusal to go unpunished would be bad for future transactions. So I make an example of the captives which serves to warn others how seriously my modest demands *must* be treated." He paused for a few seconds to allow both members of his audience to contemplate the implications of his words, then continued, "It's so much *better* for all concerned if everybody knows *exactly* where they stand in such matters, don't you think?"

"Y—Yes!" *Senora* Castrillo admitted pensively, trying to reconcile the polite speech and demeanor with the cold-blooded way in which her captor described his illegal activities.

"But why did you have to kill poor Raoul?" Teresa-Maria demanded indignantly, being less perceptive than her mother and not so aware of the true nature of the man she was addressing. "He wasn't armed and, unlike Pepe, didn't offer any resistance when you stopped our coach."

"True, young lady," Peraro conceded blandly. "While I regretted the need to do so, it was necessary and advantageous to *you*. I've always found the families of my 'guests' are more receptive to my demands if they have evidence that I'm in deadly earnest. So I considered the death of your servant would be preferable to *yourself* and your parents than, as some of my less salubrious contemporaries in this field would have done, sending your father some portion of you such as a finger, or an ear—."

"*Madre de dios!*" the girl gasped, realizing at last the full extent of the peril in which she and her mother had been situated since falling into the hands of such a man.

"I hope my frankness hasn't caused you distress, my dear young *senorita,*" Peraro said, with what passed as solicitude and gentleness, having no doubt that the conversation would be repeated to his advantage once the captives rejoined their own kind. "And now, ladies, it is time you were leaving. But, before you go, let me give you a word of *advice* to pass to Don Martin. Tell him it would be *most* unwise to attempt to take reprisals against me, either with his *vaqueros* or by reporting what has happened to the *Guardia Rurales*. Remind him that the only man foolish enough ever to do so would have come to regret his folly, had he and his family lived long enough. As it was, he died before he could see what happened to his wife and children. The men of my band, ladies, are less gentle and respectful than I when they are roused. You will remember to tell your husband this, *senora?*"

"I will," the woman promised, knowing that beneath the veneer of politeness and softly spoken words was a man completely ruthless and uncaring about the lives of other human beings. "Don Martin will do as you say!"

"Bueno," the *bandido* chief asserted and, having assisted first the daughter, then the mother—each of whom accepted his aid with reluctance and repugnance, but were too afraid of him to refuse it—into the coach, he concluded, *"Vaya con dios*. My men will ensure you arrive safely at the place I arranged for your husband to have his *vaqueros* come and meet you."

Watching as the vehicle and its escort was disappearing, Peraro smiled with satisfaction. He felt sure the two women would tell all their friends and relations of what had happened to them, including how well they had been treated and the warnings he had given about the alternatives if his demands were not met. The story, added to those spread by earlier kidnap victims, would have a salutary effect upon the families of those abducted in the future. What was more, being a good judge of human nature, he was equally certain *Senora* Castrillo would do everything in her power to dissuade her husband from putting any contemplated punitive action into effect.

Turning as the coach went out of sight beyond the buildings of the town which surrounded the *cantina,* the *bandido* chief strolled into the once more rowdy and festive barroom.

Glancing around, he noticed Florencia was missing. For a moment, being in the mood to celebrate, he thought of sending for her to join him. Then, having no doubt she was resentful of the blow and would make anything but pleasant company, he decided against doing so. Instead, he crossed to the table at which he had been playing Spanish *monte* with some of the leading members of his gang when the ransom money had arrived.

"Well, that's another one over, Ramon," Marcos Bordillo greeted, with a familiarity no other man or woman at present in the room would have dared to employ. "Were they as impressed as all the others by what you told them?"

"They were, Marcos," Peraro affirmed, his habit of imparting the warning to departing victims being well known. He showed none of the irritation he always experienced when the other addressed him by his first name, but did not precede it with the honorific "Don" which was used by everybody else—except for whoever was currently his mistress—in his hearing. "They did indeed."

In his late forties, big, corpulent to the point of obesity, as might be expected from the sedentary and lascivious life he had always lived, Bordillo was dressed as expansively as the *bandido* chief without making any effort whatsoever to keep the attire clean. Going bald on top, his longish black hair was always impregnated by an aromatic lotion of a particularly sickly kind. To help disguise the fact that he rarely washed and still more infrequently bathed all over, he also annointed himself with an equally noticeable perfume. Dark joweled and badly shaven, his face had a certain jollity—if being sufficiently porcine of features to have him known behind his back as *"el Cerdo"*, "the Pig"—but with a strong suggestion of his licentious and far from savory nature.

Serving as *alcalde,* mayor, of Escopeta alone would not have qualified Bordillo to take such a liberty with the proud and touchy *bandido* chief. He had other qualities which made him practically indispensible. Not only had he some very useful and influential political connection in Saltillo—capital city of the State of Coahuila—which offered a measure of protection for the illicit activities of the gang, but he had also frequently had access to information of value. Furthermore, he was related to a wealthy family with the power to "pull strings" at national governmental level in Mexico City itself and obtain results which were even more valuable. As a consideration for keeping him out of the way, they had proved most helpful to Peraro since the liaison was formed.

Being ill-advised in his selection of partners for sexual excesses, the other members of Bordillo's family had made arrangements for him to be settled in Escopeta. He had been sufficiently shrewd and alert to the danger to have acquired evidence of certain of their political and business activities, which would have led them to face execution if it was to fall into the wrong hands. This had ensured that they did not rid themselves of him in a more permanent fashion. They were, therefore, insistent that he must be kept alive and in what for him was good health. In addition, being aware of what their fate would be if anything should happen to *el Cerdo*, they had made certain Peraro was fully appreciative of how he personally would be affected if misfortune befell their errant kinsman.

All of which made the *bandido* chief consider that the *alcalde* was sufficiently valuable for him to accept, if not approve at heart, of such familiarity from him.

"Of course they were," Edmundo *"Culebra"* Perez declared, with the slurred speech of one who was on the verge of becoming drunk. Raising a glass filled with *mescal* in the fashion of proposing a toast, he went on, *"Nobody* can tell it the way Don Ramon does. *Saludos, patron!"*

Stocky, middle sized and a few years older than his leader, the speaker then tossed the whole of the fiery and potent liquor down his throat in a single gulp. There was something repellant, almost reptilian about him which accounted for his nickname, "Snake". He had an oak brown, heavily moustached face—etched with such lines of debauchery and evil only an exceptionally doting, or blind, mother could have loved—and spoke with a harsh, rasping voice. Despite his prominence in the gang, his clothes were those that an ordinary *vaquero* would have changed into at the end of a day's work if intending to go into town for a night of celebration. He had a plain yet very functional fighting knife sheathed on the left side of his belt and, disdaining the use of a holster, had a well used Colt Artillery Model Peacemaker thrust into it so the scarred walnut handle was available for grasping by either hand. As always, his feet were bare. There were callouses at least half an inch thick on the soles, preventing discomfort when they were in the stirrup irons of a saddle.

"It's *breeding* and family background which does the trick," Jesus[1] "Obispo" Sanchez explained, his accent and demeanor suggesting a higher social status than that of Perez. After having duplicated the action of the other, but with a glass of wine and, sipping rather than gulping it, showing less signs for approaching intoxication, he continued, "*Some* of us have it, *Culebra,* my friend. Others don't and *never* will."

Tall, lean, somewhat younger and better looking than the man he was addressing, Sanchez clearly modeled his appearance and behavior upon that of his leader; but was sufficiently intelligent to make sure he never quite achieved the same aristocratic mien and bearing. His clothing, while of excellent cut and quality, was clean, tidy, yet somber in its elegance. Also armed with a revolver and knife, the former was a Smith & Wesson New Model "Russian" rimfire in a cross-draw holster. He was completely bald, and his clean shaven face had an austere expression. This, the way he dressed, and the fact that he was a former priest unfrocked for choosing unwisely a young female parishioner with whom to have sexual intercourse resulting in her becoming pregnant, had created his sobriquet, "Bishop."

Such an indiscretion could have been smoothed over, as had happened on two previous occasions, but the girl was the illegitimate daughter of a cardinal who yielded to the demands of her adoptive mother—his sister—to take punitive action. Finding himself unemployed and seeing no

1. *Pronounced, "Hey-Soos". J. T. E.*

hope of obtaining an equally lucrative form of honest living, he had elected to become a *bandido*. Being of a sporting nature, he had taken an active interest in the use of firearms and fencing while still a man of the cloth. How well he had absorbed his lessons showed in the fact that he had not only survived in his very competitive new chosen field of endeavor, but had risen to the point where he was competing with Perez for the position of *segundo* to Peraro, and, like his rival, had ambitions to supplant the *bandido* chief.

"It's useful, as you and I know, Jesus," Peraro remarked amiably, having responded by raising his glass and taking a drink of what everybody in the barroom—even the nominal owner—believed to be *tequila*, but was in fact nothing more intoxicating than appropriately colored water. He was too wise to ever allow liquor to get the better of him in such company. "But there are other qualities just as useful in our line of work, eh, Edmundo?"

Tact rather than politeness had dictated the *bandido* chief worded the reply in such a fashion!

Aware of just how precarious a position he had attained, as he remembered how he had acquired it from his predecessor, Peraro never allowed himself to forget there was always going to be somebody willing to supplant him by the same means. Not did he exclude either of the men he had addressed so diplomatically from the possession of such an ambition. As a result of his very efficient espionage service, he knew their thoughts on the matter only too well and he used these same desires to form what might be termed a buffer state for his own protection between them. He had also learned from the same reliable sources that each preferred having him, rather than the other, as the head of the gang. They were conscious of how short an expectancy of life would lie ahead should he be replaced by one of the other of them.

Therefore, ever mindful of how much was at stake, Peraro invariably walked a delicately balanced path between the two potential candidates for his leadership. One of the tactics he employed to help bring this about was to strictly avoid showing favor openly or overtly in either direction.

He did not doubt each man had a system of spying almost as effective as his own, watching himself as well as the other for any warning suggestion of favoritism on his part.

In addition to protecting himself against Perez and Sanchez as individuals, the *bandido* chief also needed to maintain the support of both as each possessed special qualities which were valuable to him. Both were almost as unscrupulous, ruthless and competent as himself and excellent fighting men in their own right. While *Culebra* was marginally better at using a knife, *Obispo* was fractionally superior when it came to handling a revolver. The superiority in each case was so slight that neither was willing to gamble his own life upon his ability to beat the other. They both had their adherents, but neither had so many he could exert dominance upon the other faction and there were sufficient owing allegiance only to Peraro—as long as he remained in power, at any rate—for neither group to threaten the collective power of the gang as a whole.

Despite his having fallen from grace, one of the most important qualities possessed by Sanchez was the contacts he maintained within the hierarchy of the all-powerful Catholic priesthood. These offered sources of invaluable information and details of who to approach for religious assistance should it become necessary. He could also mingle undetected, generally with a wig as a disguise, in a high class of society which was closed to his rival.

Possessing none of the social graces which made the other invaluable, Perez had the ability to duplicate his powers of associating with people, but at a lower stratum of the population. Employing cruder methods, if no less effective in producing results, he could extract co-operation and support from the poorer classes who were beyond the reach of Peraro—because of his aristocratic pretensions—as well as Sanchez.

Therefore, despite knowing that each was always waiting and watching for a way in which he could be supplanted, the *bandido* chief had no desire to lose the services of either!

As long as both Perez and Sanchez were still living, Peraro knew he was equally safe from the ambitions they respectively harbored!

The leader of the *bandidos* of Escopeta was too aware of how much his own position and continued existence depended upon keeping each of his prospective usurpers alive and in good health to want anything to happen to either of them, unless it also happened to the other.

"To each his own, heh, *amigos?*" the *alcalde* declared, filling his glass with *mescal* after having emptied it in response to the toast proposed by Perez. Then, gazing owlishly around him, he went on, "Hey, where's Florencia got to?"

"She's probably gone up to her room in a sulk," Sanchez suggested in a sour tone, bitterly aware that the young woman had ousted the previous mistress which he had provided for Peraro, thus depriving him of a useful means of acquiring information. To make matters worse, he guessed Florencia was serving in a similar capacity for his rival. "From what I've seen of her, she never could stand being *told* she'd behaved badly."

"She's one pretty tough kid, for all of that," *Culebra* stated, resentful of the attempt to belittle a person he was known to sponsor. Eyeing his opponent in a truculently challenging fashion, liquor always making him quarrelsome, he continued, "I remember how she took—!"

"I feel more like playing cards than watching her *dance* right now!" Peraro put in firmly, alert as always for a possible confrontation erupting when the shorter of his would-be successors had been drinking. While he knew the showdown was inevitable, he wanted it to be at a time and place of his own choosing. The present was neither the time nor the place. If certain arrangements he had made without their knowledge came to fruition, he would need both of them, and to have the gang disrupted at this stage by internal conflict was highly undesirable. Waving his hand at the cards and money lying on the table, he went on, "So what do you say we get on with our game and leave her where she is?"

"Why not, indeed?" Bordillo supported, having been fortunate in his playing for once and wanting to make the most of his interrupted lucky streak rather than deliberately trying to help the *bandido* chief keep the peace. There was, however, an expression of lascivious anticipation on his porcine face as he continued hopefully, "But perhaps we can have her down later. With the mood she'll be in after you hitting her that way, Ramon, one wrong word will—!"

"Not tonight, Marcos!" Peraro refused, in a tone which men who knew him as well as the group around the table were aware would brook no argument. "Don't forget we should have another 'guest' coming in tomorrow and I need Florencia to take care of her."

"I hope she's not going to rob this one," Sanchez commented, throwing a mocking look at Perez.

Before the shorter of the would-be leaders of the gang could reply, there was an interruption which diverted the attention of everybody in the barroom.

CHAPTER FIVE

He Wound Up Dead

Following Tomas Acusar, the Ysabel Kid showed not the slightest suggestion of concern or perturbation as he came through the main entrance of *Bernardo's Cantina*. While he was carrying his Winchester Model of 1873 "One Of A Thousand" rifle across the crook of his left arm, it was covered by a *Pehnane* Comanche boot made from fringed buckskin and decorated with painted red, white and blue "medicine" symbols. Ostensibly, this was to give notice of his pacific intentions. The main purpose of the concealment, however, was to prevent the superlative quality of the weapon from being seen by the occupants of the barroom.

As far as appearances went, the young Mexican was far more worried than his black dressed captor about their arrival!

In fact, Acusar looked—and was—decidedly ill at ease!

Knowing the vicious temper of Don Ramon Manuel José Peraro when roused, the *bandido* was deeply disturbed by the thoughts of his possible reaction to the news which was forthcoming!

Much to his surprise and considerable relief, having discarded his knife as ordered, Acusar had found he was treated as he had been promised. It had been with great trepidation that he had watched the Kid collect the enormous James Black bowie knife from where it was embedded in the skull of his brother. After cleaning the blade on the clothing of Sebastian Montalban instead of that of the man it had killed (a gesture which did not escape the attention and gratitude of the young Mexican when he came to think about it later) the knife was merely used to cut away the shirt and expose

45

his injury to view. Producing a small buckskin pouch from his saddlebags, the Texan had set about performing effective first aid. Staunching the flow of blood from the shallow groove with the dried and powdered leaves of a witch hazel tree, carried in a tobacco tin, he had bound it skilfully with a strip of clean white cloth.

With the treatment completed, the Kid had dressed and made preparations for departure. The commotion had caused the horses of the three would-be robbers to bolt and, knowing they would not have gone far with the reins dangling, he had set out to find them. Although the Kid had neither gathered up and rendered harmless the weapons which lay around, nor took his Winchester, Acusar had not attempted to profit from what might have seemed an incautious, even foolish, lapse. His captor might have gone, but the huge white stallion remained in the clearing and was watching him in a threatening fashion. At his first movement, an innocent attempt to reach up and touch the bandaged wound, it let out a snort so charged with menace he had concluded the safest thing to do was sit as if turned to stone until its master came back.

Returning with the three horses after a few minutes, the Kid had ordered his prisoner to pick up the revolvers and knives, then fasten them in a bundle using a poncho. While this was being done, showing not the slightest concern over the possibiity of one of the Colts being turned upon him, he had taken a pencil and notepad from the saddlebag which had yielded the first aid pouch. Writing something on it, he had torn off the top sheet and placed it under a rock near his belongings. Commenting that the message was for his *amigos* who would be coming to the clearing very shortly, he had made the stallion ready for traveling. With that task completed, he had told Acusar to help him load and secure the bodies on the backs of their mounts. Much to his surprise, when the task was completed, the young Mexican had discovered the Texan intended to accompany him to Escopeta.

Setting off together, each leading a horse bearing the body of its owner, the two young men had made their way

through the woodland. It had soon become apparent to the
Mexican that, while he no longer earned his living as a
smuggler along the *Rio Bravo,* the Texan had not forgotten
the geography acquired in the pursuit of such illicit business.
He had led the way to a secret crossing place which Acusar
knew, but had not intended to make use of in his company.
Before going over, he had done something which—if the
bandido had given any thought to it instead of being engrossed solely in contemplating what lay ahead on reaching
Escopeta—might have indicated he did not intend to return
to the clearing. Rising to stand on the seat of the saddle,
with the white stallion remaining as motionless as a rock,
he had taken the body of the Canada goose from where it
was suspended by the legs on the horn and hung it concealed
in the branches of a white oak tree out of reach of any
chance passing predator. With that done, the crossing was
made.

Traveling in as nearly a straight line towards their destination as the terrain allowed, Acusar had watched his
captor. He had soon concluded that the stories he had heard
about the ability of *el Cabrito* to avoid ambushes, like those
regarding the savagely effective fighting skills, were far
from being exaggerations. Without appearing to, the black
dressed Texan had constantly remained on the alert. His
keen red hazel eyes and sharp ears had seen and heard
everything which had gone on around them. he was ably
aided in his vigilance by his big white stallion, which might
have been a wild creature instead of a domesticated beast
of burden the way it behaved. Between them, it would have
been almost impossible to approach or lie in wait without
being detected.

The precautions had proved unnecessary, but Acusar felt
sure his captor did not regret having taken them.

Meeting and seeing nobody along the way, night had
fallen before the party reached its destination. On coming
into sight of the lights of Escopeta, Acusar was given another example of how the Kid was determined to avoid
taking any unnecessary chances. Turning aside into a small
grove of cottonwood trees, he had brought them to a halt.

Having tethered the horses carrying the corpses to trees, fastening the reins instead of relying upon "ground hitching" them, the young *bandido* had received other instructions. The first had been to don his *poncho,* so that his bandaged shoulder would be hidden from view. While he was doing this, the Texan had concealed the Winchester in the Comanche medicine boot. Then they resumed the interrupted journey.

Aware that the arrival on foot of an obvious "Anglo" would attract attention, even if apparently escorted by a member of the local *bandido* community, the Kid had elected to pass through the town on horseback. The ploy had been successful. Riding between the adobe *jacales* which housed the majority of the population, he and Acusar had not been challenged by the few people who had seen them. On reaching the roughly circular *plaza,* around which the few business premises, the office of the *alcalde* and—although it was a mere affectation as there was not and never had been a law enforcement agency to occupy it—the jail house were situated, they had not gone directly to *Bernardo's Cantina.* Instead, they had left their mounts at the hitching rail of the *alcade's* office and walked the rest of the way. While doing so, the Kid had repeated the instructions on the way in which the young Mexican was to behave when they went in.

As soon as the Kid and Acusar entered, a silence so potentially ominous it could almost be felt spread across the barroom!

Drinks and other activities were postponed as every eye was turned in the direction of the newcomers!

Actually, only one of the young men was being subjected to the attention of the crowd. They all recognized Acusar as being one of them and wondered why he had arrived with the other. While *gringo* outlaws from north of the *Rio Bravo* were not unknown in Escopeta, such visitations were sufficiently infrequent to arouse interest when one put in an appearance.

However, in the case of the black dressed and well armed young Texan, many of the crowd knew that—regardless of what he had been in the past—he was no outlaw!

Pausing for a moment, as if wishing to let his eyes become accustomed to the light after having spent an extended period in the darkness outside the building, the Kid swept the barroom with a gaze which was quick yet missed little. He had no need to take the precaution against being dazzled, having waited just clear of the open front door until his vision had adjusted to the changed conditions he would encounter on entering.

Everything was pretty much as the Texas remembered from previous visits!

There were some new faces, none of which the Kid considered to be indicative of a better and less vicious character than those which had gone. Behind the counter, almost short enough to be classed as a dwarf, the nominal owner and his massive Yaqui Indian wife did not appear to have aged to any noticeable degree. Much the same applied to the man he had come to visit and the rest of the group at the table. He doubted whether the passage of time had reduced the ability of any one of them as fighting men. The fact that all were still alive was convincing evidence to support the supposition.[1]

Giving Acusar a gentle shove with his right hand, having told of his intentions on entering and informing him what he expected to be done, the Texan stepped forward. On the receipt of the signal, the young *bandido* led the way towards the table occupied by his leader. It was obvious to all the onlookers that something was amiss and that he was not looking forward to what he anticipated would be forthcoming when the events of earlier in the day were reported to Don Ramon.

---

1. *We realize that the names of the town and* cantina, *the description of its nominal owner and other details differ from those given in* Part Three, the Ysabel Kid *in* "Sam Ysabel's Son", THE TEXAN. *This is due to there having been discrepancies in the information from which we produced the original manuscript. These have now been corrected via a study of documents presented to us by Alvin Dustine "Cap" Fog, for whom we also have the honor of being biographer. See series of the same name. J. T. E.*

On the other hand, the Texan seemed completely at ease. For all the concern he was exhibiting, he clearly considered himself among—if not exactly *friends*—at least people who would treat him with hospitality.

Yet, for all his apparent relaxation, the Kid was as alert as a cougar scenting danger and just as ready to take sudden, violent action should the need arise!

At every succeeding step he was taking, the Texan was conscious of the avaricious and calculating way in which he was being scrutinized. The occupants of the room were taking everything in and estimating the value of all he carried upon his person. With the possible exception of Peraro, Jesus *"Obispo"* Sanchez and Marcos *"el Cerdo"* Bordillo, there was hardly a person present who would have hesitated before killing him for his clothing, the old Colt Model of 1848 Dragoon revolver, the bowie knife and his rifle, if granted an opportunity. What was more, should the *bandido* chief or his sombrely dressed would-be successor learn the true nature of the rifle concealed by the *Pehnane* medicine boot, he would not exclude even them from trying to gain possession of it.

However, as the Kid had anticipated, nobody attempted to molest him as he continued to stroll with such seeming nonchalance across the room. Everybody was waiting to see how Don Ramon reacted to his arrival. There was, in all probability, not a single person present who had missed witnessing at least one example of how their leader responded to any flouting of his authority. Even if there were any of them present who had missed such a demonstration in the past, he would already have ben warned of what happened to those who were sufficiently ill-advised to make the attempt.

Therefore, in spite of being ready in case he was required to defend himself, the Texan did not envisage there would be any need for him to do so *before* he had concluded the conversation with Peraro!

"Saludos, Don Ramon," the Kid greeted in his fluent border Spanish, as he and his prisoner—which, to the experienced gaze of the men at the table, was the status of

the frightened looking young Mexican regardless of there being no visible form of restraint—came to a halt in front of the man to whom the words were addressed.

"*Saludos, Cabrito,*" Peraro replied, studying Acusar for a moment with a baleful gaze which did nothing to create a sense of peace of mind for its recipient. Then he turned his attention to the black clad Texan and delivered a calculating examination. He was certain only a matter of the greatest importance would have warranted the visit. This was no mere act of *braggadocio,* provoked by a dare or bet from the honest cowhands with whom *el Cabrito* was now associating. Even with the *very* important connections he possessed on both sides of the international border, he would have needed a much stronger and more serious motive before coming to Escopeta. Therefore, the *bandido* leader considered it advisable to learn more and went on, "This is an *unexpected* surprise. May I ask what brings you to see me?"

"I've got bad news, *senor,*" the Texan replied with polite formality, then gestured over his shoulder with his head. "Only don't let me keep all these good folks from their enjoyment."

"Carry on with your drinking, my children," the *bandido* leader shouted, taking the hint. "Our friend Bernardo can't get rich if he isn't selling anything, can he?"

"I can't get rich anyway," the nominal owner stated to his wife but was wise enough to ensure the words reached only her ears. "Not with that fancy talking son-of-a-whore taking all the 'mother-something' profits."

"Like I said, *senor,*" the Kid drawled, declining the offer of a seat at the table, as the interrupted activities of the other occupants were continued, albeit at a reduced level and with every indication that their main attention was upon himself and the reason for his visit. "Your nephew, this *hombre* and his brother tried to rob me north of the *Rio Bravo* this morning."

"The god-damned *fools!*" Peraro ejaculated furiously.

"It wasn't close to being the *smartest* thing they could've done, way things turned out," the Texan admitted. "Of course, to be fair all 'round, they likely didn't know at first it was *my* gear they were fixing to help themselves to."

"W—We d—di—didn't, *p-pa—patron!*" Acusar confirmed, his speech being impaired somewhat by an inability to prevent his teeth chattering with terror as the savage gaze of his leader was swung back in his direction. "And, when I guessed from the clothes, rifle and horse who it was, neither Alfredo nor 'Tian—I mean Sebastian—!"

"I know *who* you meant!" Peraro growled. "Go on with your story!"

"I—I tried to tell them," the young Mexican concluded hurriedly, after giving an accurate description of the events preceding the arrival of the Kid. "But neither of them would listen to me. They were too busy arguing about who had what."

"Which is about all I'd expect of *either* of them!" the *bandido* chief claimed in tones of derision. "But how do you mean about recognizing the clothes and rifle, didn't *Cabrito* have them with him?"

"N—No!" Acusar gasped. "H—They—We—!"

"What the hell does he mean, *Cabrito?*" Peraro inquired, but less savagely, looking at the black clad Texan in an interrogative fashion. "I can't get any 'mother-something' sense out of *him!*"

"I didn't conclude they'd stop doing it was I to have asked and me with only this old toad-sticker to hand for backing it up," the Kid asserted, when he had explained about the successful hunt for the Canada goose. "And, soon's I saw his brother was figuring to shoot that old Blackie hoss of mine—Well, I reckon I don't need to tell *you* what *that* did to me, way you feel about that big black *Diablo* stallion of yours."

"You *don't!*" Peraro affirmed definitely. "But the good *Diablo* is no more, *Cabrito.*"

"I'm right sorry to hear that, *senor,*" the Texan claimed, with genuine sympathy. "Was it an accident?"

"Nothing more than old age and, before he died, he left me a son who is at least his equal," the *bandido* chief explained and his pride was obvious. "Anyway, under such conditions, I can't blame you for stopping Acusar." He paused and glanced around, then went on, "By the way, where are those two other fools?"

"I took out Afredo, I reckon his name was, with my knife."

"And Sebastian?"

"He threw down on me and missed, so he wound up dead as well."

"That's understandable," Peraro conceded, his face giving no indication of how he was receiving the news from the person responsible that a kinsman had been killed. His eyes were diverted to deliver a look which caused the recipient to cower as if expecting a blow at the very least, and he continued in a scathing voice, "But *this* one seems to have come through safely."

"Just a nick, way it turned out, but he'd've died like the others had he been *loco* enough to try to fight on after he'd took it," the Kid replied. "I had him keep his wound covered while we was riding through town, so's nobody'd see it and make a mistake. I'll tell you something else, though. He was way out the smartest of the three, no matter your nephew was one of them. Like he told you, he figured out who they was fixing to rob, but those other two knobheads just wouldn't listen when he tried to give them a warning."

"That's about what I'd expect of Sebastian," Peraro confessed. "And something in young Acusar's favor. By the way, *Cabrito*, he was only the son of a second cousin who I never really liked. Not that I'm especially bothered, but where is he?"

"We left him and the other *hombre* in that cottonwood grove just outside town," the Kid replied, concluding he had been told the truth by Acusar about the relationship between the *bandido* chief and Montalban. "Like I told you, I didn't want to draw no notice and questions on the way here."

"Why *did* you come? demanded Edmundo *"Culebra"* Perez.

"Because it was the *honorable* thing for a man to do," the Kid asserted, knowing enough about conditions among the *bandidos* to believe such a response would give Sanchez an excuse to support him, and making it plain he was directing the explanation solely to the inquirer who would not understand such a matter as honor. As *Obispo* nodded in approval and agreement, he went on, "I don't know whether Don Ramon sent those three out or not, 'cepting I wouldn't reckon he'd trust them four inches out of his sight without somebody to wet-nurse them. But I do know he'd want to find out the why of it when they didn't come back. Which I concluded to save him the need and trouble to do it and, by coming personal, making sure he heard the straight of it." Having delivered the statement, without waiting for a response, he turned his gaze to the young Mexican and asked, "Well, is that how things went?"

"It is, *patron!*" Acusar confirmed without hesitation, grateful for the way in which he had been shown in a better light than his brother and Montalban. "*Cabrito* has spoken the truth about everything."

"You were riding alone, *Cabrito?*" Peraro wanted to know, speaking with what appeared to be no more than casual interest.

"Nope," the Kid lied, but with such conviction he might have been speaking the unvarnished truth. "Cap'n Fog, Mark Counter and Waco were going to meet me at the clearing. Fact being, they'll likely be there and waiting by now. I left them a note telling where I was headed and why."

"Most wise," the *bandido* chief praised, after looking at and having received a nod of confirmation from Acusar who—although unaware that the men for whom the message was supposed to be intended were nowhere in the vicinity nor likely to be—had seen the precaution taken. "And I'm grateful to you for being so considerate."

"Like I said, Don Ramon, it was the honorable thing to do way I saw it," the Kid answered, speaking so loudly his words carried around the barroom to the occupants who were all listening to the conversation regardless of what they had been told by their leader. "And now, I'm asking whether you hold me any grudge for what those three of your men left me no choice but to do?"

Once again, an ominous silence came upon the barroom.

More than ever since the arrival of the two young men, the occupants were giving their undevoted attention to the table of their leader!

Everybody was waiting to hear the reply made by the *bandido* chief!

That included the Kid!

All too well the black clad young Texan realized he would soon know his fate!

Depending upon the answer given by Peraro, the Kid could leave unmolested and in safety!

Or be compelled to try and fight his way out, with small chance of succeeding against such odds!

CHAPTER SIX

Who's Going to Kill Me

There was a pause, which seemed to be dragging on interminably to the occupants of the barroom in *Bernardo's Cantina*, while Ramon Manuel José Peraro was considering how he should reply.

As the *bandido* leader was always aware, in the kind of society to which he belonged, it was more than merely inadvisable for it to be considered that he had made a wrong decision. It could prove fatal and would, at the very least, weaken his authority over the remainder of the gang. Unless rapidly and forcibly checked, the latter was almost certain to result in the former.

Peraro knew the three names mentioned by the Ysabel Kid!

Every one was a peerless fighting man in his own right, but this was not the point uppermost at that moment in the mind of the *bandido* leader. He was taking into account that no less a person than President Sebastian Lerdo de Tejas of Mexico had been saved by them from assassination.[1] *El Presidente* had acquired a well deserved reputation for repaying his debts and supporting those who had done him services. Furthermore, many influential people in Mexico would remember how *el Cabrito* had helped Captain Dustine Edward Marsden "Dusty" Fog to deliver a vitally important shipment of repeating rifles to Benito Juarez. This had caused the defection of a large number of former Confederate soldiers from "Emperor" Ferdinand Joseph Maximillian, the would-be ruler appointed by the French, and had played a

1. *Told in:* THE PEACEMAKERS. *J. T. E.*

considerable part in having him overthrown and executed.[2]

Even if he had liked his kinsman rather than regarding him as a nuisance and an incompetent, Peraro would have hesitated before attempting to seek revenge upon a person so well connected as the Ysabel Kid. Therefore, under the conditions which prevailed and particularly in view of his plans for the immediate future, he was disinclined to take the chance of arousing the hostility and animosity of so many powerful people.

However, the references to the "honorable" aspects of the situation offered the *bandido* leader a way out of the dilemma. It was always his pose to be a man of unshakable principles, which would permit him to accept that another was of the same high moral standards. Nor was it likely anybody would raise an argument if he should make his decision on such grounds.

"I agree that you acted in the only way possible under the circumstances, *Cabrito,* and as I, or anybody else here, would have done in your place," Peraro affirmed, in a carrying tone similar to that with which the question had been asked. "The fault was all theirs and you did no more than you had to do. I neither attach fault to you, nor hold any grudge whatsoever."

"*Bueno, gracias,*" the black clad young Texan declared and meant it. "Which being the case, I'll be headed back to meet up with Cap'n Fog and the boys."

"Straight away?" the *bandido* chief asked, with what might have been solicitude and disappointment. "Can't we offer you a drink, or food?"

"Neither, *gracias,*" the Kid refused, but in such a polite manner it offered no offense. "I'd food along with me and ate on the way down here. So seeing's how we're headed for a meeting with some important folks up to Eagle Pass, I'd best not keep Cap'n Fog waiting any longer than need be."

"You know best and are to be commended on being so conscientious," Peraro assented and praised. "Goodbye then,

2. *Told in:* THE YSABEL KID. *J. T. E.*

Cabrito. And, once again, my thanks for your consideration in this matter."

"Like I said, it was the honorable thing to do," the Texan drawled. "Happen it's all right with you, I'll take this young feller along to bring the bodies in."

"Do as you wish, *Cabrito,*" the *bandido* chief authorized, before directing a far less hostile glance at Tomas Acusar than had previously been the case. "Unless his wound is troubling him too much, that is."

"I'll be all right, *patron,*" the young Mexican claimed, relieved by the indication that he was not being held responsible for the death of Sebastian Montalban.

"Are you going to let the half-breed get away with it, *jefe?*" inquired Edmundo *"Culebra"* Perez, employing a term which was equally applicable to himself, after the Kid and Acusar had left the barroom and conversation was welling up all around.

"I am," Peraro replied. "You heard what he said about having left a note telling Fog where he was going and what he intended to do."

"Do you think he did leave one?" Perez asked.

"Perhaps he did, perhaps he was only bluffing," answered the *bandido* chief. "But I've given him my word that I don't hold him a grudge and I won't break it."

"That wouldn't be the honorable thing to do, *Culebra,*" pointed out Jesus *"Obispo"* Sanchez. "And everybody knows Don Ramon is a man of honor."

"Just where the hell do you think you're going?" demanded Conrado Delgado, stepping from behind a bush with his Spencer carbine held ready for use to confront the man he had heard approaching. He had been just about to go on foot to carry out the assignment he had been given.

"What's it to you?" challenged Enrique Obtener, halting and beginning to turn forward the barrel of the equally old Henry rifle in his hands.

While each man was wearing the attire of a working *vaquero,* neither had ever been employed in that or any other legitimate occupation. They were, in fact, *bandidos* from birth and choice, both having a mutually acute antipathy to any form of sweat-raising labor. Each was currently a member of the gang led by Ramon Peraro. For all that, the first speaker gave more of his loyalty to Jesus Sanchez and the second was an equally whole-hearted adherent of Edmundo Perez.

According to the old adage, great minds have a habit of thinking alike!

The minds of *Obispo* and Culebra, while devious, could hardly be termed great by any stretch of the imagination. In spite of this, their thoughts had run along almost identical lines after the departure of the Ysabel Kid from *Bernardo's Cantina*. Before many minutes had elapsed, each had seen a way in which he believed he might be able to ingratiate himself with their leader. In one respect, it had been Sanchez who inadvertently supplied the suggestion of how this might be brought about to his hated rival. His comment about the honorable ways of Peraro had set both to thinking. How closely their cogitations had run along parallel lines was demonstrated by the meeting of the two men in the woodland some eight miles north and slightly east of Escopeta.

Excusing himself, when the suggestion was made by Marcos *"el Cerdo"* Bordillo for the game of Spanish *monte* to be resumed, ostensibly to answer the call of nature, *Obispo* had crossed the room as if meaning to do so. On his way, he had selected his intended agent with great care. He had at least three men in his entourage who possessed qualities which might have made any one seem the logical choice, but he did not pick any of them. Being newly arrived and not yet known as an out and out adherent, Delgado had struck him as ideal. Seeing the surreptitious signal from the man he considered his actual leader, the newcomer had followed him from the *cantina*. Finding a spot in the darkness where they could talk without the danger of being overheard, Sanchez had given his instructions. As he had anticipated, the newcomer was sufficiently brave, but not intelligent enough to question the reason, for carrying out the orders.

On his return, *Obispo* had found Perez was absent. Such

was his contempt for the intelligence of his rival, he had
not suspected the departure was to do with anything other
than bring relief to a set of bowels over flowing with *mescal*.
Yet the purpose of *Culebra* had been identical to his own.
Furthermore, in spite of having adherents of longer standing
and who might have been more capable, he had too chosen
a newcomer to act on his behalf.

Following the advice he had been given by Sanchez,
Delgado had set off in the direction of the secret crossing
by which the Ysabel Kid and Tomas Acusar had entered
Mexico. Unknown to him, Obtener had left a couple of
minutes later. Over the years, as the adherents of the three
factions began to settle in their respective groups for mutual
support and protection—except for those living among and
spying upon the opposition—the town had become split
into three sections. Therefore, leaving from their respective
areas, they had traveled parallel to and on opposite sides of
the trail which led to the crossing. Being aware of the kind
of man they were stalking, although neither was willing to
accept any *gringo*—even one with *Indio* blood—could be
anywhere nearly as good as claimed, each had taken pre-
cuations against being seen or heard from other than a short
distance. Aided by the open woodland of the terrain they
were traversing, each had done this so effectively that the
other had remained unaware of his presence in the vicinity
while riding along.

Having covered about half the distance to the *Rio Bravo*
with nothing to disturb his belief that he was the only hunter
for *el Cabrito*, Delgado had seen a flickering red glow
among the bushes not far ahead. Although he was still too
far away to be able to discover who was near the campfire,
he felt certain he had located his quarry. There was, to the
best of his knowledge, nobody else in the vicinity. Telling
himself that the ease with which he had found the black
clad Texan was proof that all the stories he had heard were
grossly exaggerated, he had nevertheless decided against
riding any closer.

Dismounting and fastening his horse to a bush, Delgado
had been on the point of commencing his stalk when he

heard enough to warn him that he was not alone in the woodland. Taking cover, he had waited until the other traveler was close enough to be identified. It was not, as he had envisaged at first, *el Cabrito* who had somehow contrived to get behind him. Instead, the newcomer was a man of his own race. He remembered having seen the other around Escopeta, but not in the same company as he kept.

Which meant the newcomer belonged to one of the other factions!

Knowing something of the internal politics of the gang, Delgado had believed that the second *bandido* was part of the group which gave its complete loyalty to Peraro. Sharing his superior's low impression of the intellect of *Culebra*, he could not believe a mission similar to his own would have been instigated from that source. In spite of his summation, however, he was annoyed by the arrival of the other man. He had been promised a sizeable reward for carrying out the assignment and had no wish to be deprived of it by an interloper.

Equally unsuspecting the possibility of outside interference until the moment when they faced each other, Obtener was no more enamoured than Delgado at the discovery that he was not the only *bandido* hunting *el Cabrito*. Despite the instinctive response with his Henry rifle, he too drew an erroneous conclusion regarding the loyalties of the man who stepped from the bushes. It was, he concluded, unlikely that *Obispo* would care sufficiently about the affront placed upon their *patron* to try to have it avenged. However, he was to receive a sizeable gratuity from his *jefe* for killing the man responsible and was most displeased by the possibility of having somebody around who might interfere with him as he went to do so.

"Don Ramon sent me aft—!" Delgado began, but had just sufficient presence of mind to hold down his voice.

"Don Ramon told me to—!" Obtener commenced at the same moment, also taking the precaution of speaking softly.

"So you are from the *patr*—!" the lanky supporter of Sanchez ejaculated, before he could stop himself.

"What did Don Ramon send y—?" the equally scrawny

adherent of Perez started to inquire, then he too realized he was being indiscreet.

Once again, both sets of words trailed off as each speaker began to appreciate the true state of affairs!

It has become apparent to the men that neither had been sent by Peraro!

It was a situation that neither *bandido* had envisaged!

Nor did either man feel it improved matters when the understanding of what was portended by the discovery struck home!

"God damn it!" Delgado spat out indignantly, yet still retaining just enough control to continue speaking almost as quietly. Starting to move his Spencer carbine back to the position of readiness from which he had allowed it to sag, he went on, "You're one of that 'mother something' *Culebra's* men!"

"And you're for that miserable son-of-a-whore fallen priest, *Obispo!*" Obtener accused with equal vehemence, although he too was alert to the danger and refrained from raising his voice. "The *patron* didn't send *you!*"

"He didn't send you, either!" Delgado pointed out with some justification. "And, seeing I was here first, I'm going to take out *Cabrito!*"

"Like shit you are!" Obtener stated, crouching slightly. "Don Edmundo sent me to do it and—!"

"*Don Edmundo!*" snorted the Sanchez adherent derisively. "Since when does that goddamned half breed give orders?"

"He's got as much right to give them as that 'mother-something' fallen priest of yours has!" claimed the Perez supporter. "And I'm going to do what he told me!"

"Like 'something' you are!" Delgado asserted. "That's what *I'm* here to do and *nobody* is going to stop me!"

"I wish you two bastards would make up your minds who's going to kill me, then maybe I can get some sleep!"

Apparently coming from the blackness thrown by the branches of a white oak tree about twenty feet from where the conversation was taking place, the comment was delivered in English!

Although each *bandido* had forgotten caution and was

gradually speaking louder as tempers rose, they heard what was said!

Possessing no other language except that of their own country, neither Delgado nor Obtener understood the comment!

Both realized who must have spoken!

There was unlikely to be any other foreigner in the woodland!

Which meant the speaker must be the man who Sanchez and Perez had respectively sent the pair to kill!

"It's *Cabrito!*" Delgado yelled in alarm, an instinct for self preservation overriding thoughts of inter-gang hostilities.

"Over there!" Obtener shouted, also forgetting rivalry in the stress of the moment, swinging his Henry towards the shadows beneath the white oak.

Moving almost as quickly as his erstwhile antagonist, their emnity discarded in the face of mutual peril, Delgado snapped the butt of the Spencer to his right shoulder. He too had estimated the position from which the voice originated, but was unable to see anything of the speaker. Concluding this was because of the Indian dark features and all black clothing of their intended victim (as Obtener was also deducing) he sighted and squeezed off a shot.

The deep bellow of the heavier discharge from the .52 calibre carbine echoed the sharper crack given by the twenty-eight grains of black powder from the .44 caliber cartridge in the Henry rifle!

Two bullets thudded into something!

However, the sounds indicated that whatever had been hit was considerably more solid than human flesh!

Confirmation that the attempt to kill the Kid had failed was very quickly forthcoming!

"You guessed wrong!" the mocking voice warned, speaking Spanish, but it now came from a spot some feet from the white oak.

Instantly and with profanely startled exclamations, the two *bandidos* began to turn their weapons in the appropriate direction!

While doing so, each man was making ready to fire again

at the still unseen Texan!

Of the pair, Obtener was the better equiped to complete the recharging of an empty chamber!

Which proved unfortunate for the supporter of Perez!

Having estimated the type of weapons being employed against him, being guided by the different sounds of the detonations, the Kid had no doubt which assailant would pose the greatest danger to him. While both were using repeaters, because of the systems by which the respective mechanisms functioned, the Henry was much faster to re-load than the Spencer. With each, moving the lever up and down served to eject the spent case and replace it with the next loaded cartridge from the tubular magazine regardless of the different positions of this aid to continuous fire.[3] However, there was a divergence of vital importance from that point in the operation. Before the Spencer could be discharged again, it had to be cocked manually. Where the "grandfather" of the Winchester Model of 1873 carried by the Texan was concerned, the mechanism for reloading caused the hammer to be cocked at the same time.

Already cradling the Winchester in the firing position, the Kid swung its barrel to take aim with the speed and skill which had enabled him to win it against very stiff opposition at the First Cochise County Fair.[4] He knew his would-be killers were likely to be at least partially dazzled by the muzzle blast from their weapons. That was why he had spoken from his actual position without employing the al-most ventriloquial quality learned as a child.[5] By doing so, he was hoping to create confusion for the short time he needed to follow through his proposed line of action.

Having aligned the rifle on where he guessed the chest

---

3. *As was the case with the majority of its successors from the Winchester Repeating Firearms Company, the magazine tube of the Henry rifle— holding fifteen cartridges—was underneath and as long as the barrel. Having a capacity of seven rounds, that of the Spencer was in the butt. J.T.E.*

4. *Told in:* GUN WIZARD. *J. T. E.*

5. *Details of the childhood of the Ysabel Kid are given in:* COMANCHE. *J. T. E.*

of the man with the Henry to be, such was his faith in his
skill, the Kid closed his eyes as his forefinger was completing the pressure needed to liberate the sear from the set
trigger. The Winchester barked, emitting a sudden red glow,
but his vision was not affected. Throwing the lever through
the reloading cycle, he heard the distinctive thud of a bullet
penetrating the chest cavity as he was lunging aside. By the
time he halted, there was the crash of something heavy
falling and the kind of rustling that is caused by limbs
thrashing in mindless agony.

For all his speed, the Texan had only just moved swiftly
enough!

Despite his eyesight having been somewhat impaired by
the eruption of light as he and Obtener fired, Delgado wasted
no time in responding to the threat. Halting the movement
of the Spencer, he touched off a shot an instant after the
man by his side was hit. By chance more than skilled lining
of the sights, the heavy bullet passed through the space
which his intended victim had only just vacated. Without
waiting to discover whether he was successful nor not, he
snatched down the triggerguard lever of the carbine.

Once again the red hazel eyes of the Kid peered along
the barrel of the Winchester. It cracked seven times, the
lever being worked with such rapidity that the detonations
formed a continuous roll of a drum rather than forming
separate sounds. Nevertheless, he was moving the barrel
fractionally in the brief intervals that the lever was being
manipulated. Spreading out like the ribs of a fan, instead
of following one another in Indian file, the bullets engulfed
the man at whom they were being directed so effectively.
No less than four of them ploughed into his torso, sending
him flying from his feet. The Spencer, with its action still
open, left his hands as he was falling and they both landed
on the ground at almost the same moment.

Once more, the Texan changed position as soon as he
had finished firing. Although he took shelter behind a tree
which was sufficiently sturdy to halt any further lead sent
at him, none came. Instead, there was only the decreasing
volume of the thrashing from where his first victim had

fallen and the hoarse sound known as a "death rattle" originating at the point where the other *bandido* had gone down.

Both noises soon died away!

Despite the suggestion that he had succeeded in dealing with both his assailants, the Kid was too experienced a fighting man to take unnecessary chances. Instead of leaving his position of safety when the sounds came to an end, he remained where he was. Watching and listening for any indication that one or the other *bandido* was only pretending to be dead, he also gave thought to what could have led to the attempt upon his life.

A desire to avoid possible trouble and danger to the Anglo and *Chicano* population in the area of the fight in the clearing, rather than a sense of honor, had caused the Kid to visit Escopeta. He had known that even killing Tomas Acusar and burying all three bodies would not have been sufficient to prevent some kind of reprisal from taking place. When Sebastian Montalban and the brothers did not return, Peraro would have sent men to look for them. Knowing Mexican *bandidos* as well as he did, the Texan felt certain they would not merely restrict themselves to carrying out a search. They would go on a looting expedition and, when doing so north of the Rio Grande, it was not their habit to leave behind living witnesses.

Therefore, the Kid had gambled on the pretence of Peraro to be a man of honor to prevent such a search and raid being made. Although he had never heard the term, he was counting upon playing to the ego of the *bandido* leader, not only to preserve the potential victims from a foray, but also to allow him to leave the town alive. However, regardless of having achieved this, he had not allowed himself to believe he was completely safe. Being aware of the possibility, he had taken steps to circumvent any attempt made upon his life. Selecting an area from which the light of a campfire would be seen, he had baited the trap and, hearing his would be attackers approaching, had gone to spring it with all the deadly skill of a name warrior of the *Pehnane* Comanche's famed Dog Soldier war lodge. Although he had heard enough to believe that the two *bandidos* were not acting upon the orders of their leader, but had been sent by Sanchez and Peréz who had each hoped to score off the other, he was now faced with how to handle the latest development. After giving the matter his consideration, he felt sure he could produce an acceptable solution.

Five minutes went by, during which there was no movement whatsoever from the two mounds on the ground. Then, regardless of his belief that both were dead, he took the Winchester in his left hand and drew the Colt Dragoon revolver with the right, as being easier to wield at close quarters, before leaving his place of concealment.

"Damn it to hell!" the Kid growled under his breath, thinking of the wager in which he was involved with other members of the OD Connected ranch's floating outfit. Then, as he was advancing warily, he grinned and went on just as quietly, "I wonder if I can say this fuss, being down in Mexico, don't count as getting into trouble?"

CHAPTER SEVEN

I Wouldn't Advise You to Try

Panting for breath, Don Ramon Manuel José Peraro rolled tiredly from the naked and profusely perspiring body of Florencia Cazador. Entwining her arms and legs about him, she sought to prevent him from doing so. As he pulled to free himself from her grasp, he was willing to concede that he had never met her match as a bed mate. For all that, there were times when he found her enthusiasm for making love too demanding. Despite the blow he had given her earlier, or perhaps because of it, this was one of those occasions. Satisfying her lust when she was in such a mood was beyond him. Therefore, as she writhed around to press her hot mouth against his in a savagely passion filled kiss, and tried to tear at his bare back with fingernails that experience had taught him to insist were kept too short to scratch, he was more relieved than annoyed at hearing an urgent pounding at the door.

Wondering who would be calling at such an hour, the *bandido* chief shoved the girl away. Being too wise to resist at such a moment, she restricted herself to a hiss of annoyance over the interruption to her pleasure and untangled her limbs. Liberated, he thrust aside the covers and rose. Concealing his nakedness beneath a scarlet silk dressing gown from the chair at the side of the bed, he picked up his Colt Civilian Model Peacemaker before crossing the room.

"Who's there?" Peraro snapped, taking the precaution of standing to the side and not directly in front of the door while speaking.

"It's only me, *patron*," replied the croaking and unmistakable voice of Bernardo. "I've got something to tell you!"

"Can't it wait until morning?" Peraro demanded.

"It's pretty important," was the reply.

"Oh, very well then!" the *bandido* chief growled. Opening the door, but not offering to invite his visitor into the main bedroom of the luxuriously furnished suite of living quarters he maintained on the second floor of *Bernardo's Cantina* and where his kidnap victims were also housed, he went on coldly, "What is it?"

"I know what you said down in the barroom to *Cabrito, patron,*" answered the nominal owner of the establishment, waving a hand in the direction of the floor below. "But I figured you didn't really want him to get away with killing young Montalban and Cousin Alfredo, so I sent Cousin Gomez after him."

"You did *what?*" Peraro inquired, but with more curiosity than anger in his voice despite suspecting Bernardo had been more interested in avenging the death of Alfredo Acusar than that of Sebastian Montalban.

"I sent Cousin Gomez after him," the little man repeated, reading the emotions of his leader correctly and not in the least put out by the conversation being carried out with the revolver still in the other's hand. "Him being part Yaqui, I reckoned he was the best man to do it."

"He would be," Peraro conceded, but he clearly had reservations on the matter.

"It's all right, *patron,*" Bernardo said reassuringly, guessing correctly what was causing the suggestion of doubt in the tone of his leader. "I told Cousin Pepe to go to the stable and keep watch over *Diablo Joven* while he was away."

"*Bueno!*" Peraro praised, satisfied that the precaution he always took of having a reliable and trustworthy man stand guard over his highly prized black stallion, "Young Devil", had not been neglected in the desire for vengeance against the Ysabel Kid. "Did Gomez get him?"

"No, *patron*. There were two other *hombres* with the same idea."

"*Two* more?"

"Two, *patron.*"

"Well I'm *damned!*" Peraro ejaculated. "I didn't think

those three young fools had even one friend in Escopeta outside of each other. Or was it Tomas and another of your kin who'd gone after him without telling you?"

"No, *patron*," Bernardo replied, "none of them would dare."

"Then who the 'something' was it?" the *bandido* chief growled, patience never having been one of his virtues.

"Delgado and Obtener," the little man replied, possessing a remarkable memory when it came to the names and activities of the other members of the gang. "It looks like *Obispo* and *Culebra* both had the same idea, those two being tied in with them. Cousin Gomez was heading for the secret crossing when he heard plenty of shooting ahead. So, as one of the Winchesters that were being used was the last to fire, he went on slower and met them coming back."

"So they'd got *Cabrito?*" Peraro suggested, but in a tone which implied more doubt than hope.

"No, patron," Bernardo replied, with less sorrow than would have been the case had he been unaware of the state of affairs between the various factions of the gang. "It was more the other way around. They were both hanging over their saddles, shot dead."

"I can't say I'm sorry to hear *that,*" the *bandido* chief confessed frankly and viciously. "It will save me having to have them shot. What about *Cabrito?*"

"Cousin Gomez knew there wouldn't be any chance of getting to him now he was ready for it," the little man answered, sounding as if he thoroughly endorsed the conclusion—which he did—and holding out a folded sheet of paper. "This was tucked in the hat band of the *hombre Obispo* sent."

"Turn up the lamp and fetch it here for me, Florencia," Peraro called over his shoulder. After the girl had done so, without troubling to cover her nakedness or trying to keep out of sight of the caller, he took and read the message. It was printed in English, by a hand which only very rarely found the need to do any writing. Having finished, he asked, "Do either you or Gomez know what this says?"

"No, *patron*," Bernardo replied, tearing his gaze with reluctance from studying the voluptous curvaceous and naked body of the young woman. "I can only read Spanish and Cousin Gomez never learned how to read at all. May I ask what it says?"

"Of course," the *bandido* chief assented, showing no resentment over his mistress having been subjected to such a lascivious scrutiny and having no reason to doubt the explanation given by the nominal owner of the *cantina*. Being pleased with the general content of the message, he was only too willing to continue, "It says, 'Dear Don Ramon, I know you are a man of honor and did not send the two men I had to kill after me. So I will be—,' I believe the word is, 'obliged'—'if you will tell *Obispo* and *Culebra* I know who did send them and, should anybody else be sent, I will come to Escopeta and thank them personally. I don't think they will enjoy me having to do this.' It is signed, 'Loncey Dalton Ysabel'."[1]

"Who?" Bernardo inquired, looking like a puzzled particularly evil gnome.

"That's *Cabrito's* real name," Peraro explained, his manner far less inhospitable than at the start of the conversation in spite of still refraining from allowing the bearer of the message to enter the bedroom. "Have you forgotten he was the son of Big Sam Ysabel?"

"I had for a minute," the little man admitted, most of his attention being directed at Florencia who was still making no attempt to move beyond his range of vision. Being aware of the state of affairs which existed between his leader, Jesus *"Obispo"* Sanchez and Edmundo *"Culebra"* Perez, he went on, "It's a pity in one way Cousin Gomez didn't keep after him, except that I wouldn't want to lose him."

"Or me," the *bandido* chief admitted, being aware of the loyalty shown by the man in question.

"Hey though!" Bernardo ejaculated, struck by a remembrance. "Did you send Matteo Cantrell and five of the boys after *Cabrito*, *patron*?"

"No. Why?"

---

1. *Having seen examples, we consider it highly unlikely the Ysabel Kid wrote the message as grammatically as it was translated by Don Ramon Manuel José Peraro. J. T. E.*

"I saw them riding out as I was coming up here."

"God! Is that the time?"

"I don't know what you mean, *patron.*"

"They aren't going after *Cabrito,*" Peraro explained. "I've sent them to collect that *gringo* girl I told you to have the guest room made ready for."

"Oh, yes, now I remember," the little man said, nodding as comprehension dawned. "I hope they don't run across him then, or he might think that you've sent them after him."

"I don't think so," Peraro stated, in a manner which indicated he considered the subject did not warrant further discussion. "And, if I know him, he'll hear them coming soon enough to keep well out of their way."

"What are you going to do about *Obispo* and *Culebra* going against your orders that way, *patron?*" Bernado wanted to know, having two cousins who he believed would be more satisfactory sub-leaders from his point of view if the errant pair were to be desposed. He also found the sight of the naked girl far too enjoyable to want the conversation brought to an end, so he continued, "They're both getting too damned big for their boots and that could be dangerous."

"I'll see to them when the time comes," the *bandido* chief promised. He had reached a similar conclusion with regards to the way in which the two men had gone against his orders but he concluded that the matter must be held in abeyance until after the next kidnapping had been carried out. There was, he told himself silently as he started to close the door, a chance that the situation could be rectified and in a manner which would not alienate the adherents of either *Obispo* or *Culebra* if everything went as planned. Nodding to the little man, he finished, "But it isn't time *yet,* old friend. Right now, though, I'm sure Pepita will be waiting for you. My thanks for bringing me the news and message from *Cabrito*. Goodnight."

"Land's sakes, Mavis-gal!" Hettie Bonaparte declared, watching the young woman climb out of the fringed topped Surrey in which they had ridden from the town of Wet Slim to a small clearing some five miles east along the Rio Grande. "If you ain't the 'keep fittingest' thing I ever did see!"

"Taking some exercise each day wouldn't do *you* any harm, Aunt Hettie," replied Mavis Dearington with a smile, her accent indicating she was well educated and came from New England. Looking around at the massive, grey haired and somberly attired black woman who had been her nurse and companion from the day she was born, she went on in a tone redolent of much respect and genuine affection, "It would take off some of your weight if you did."

Tall, slender and willowy, without being flat chested or anyway boyish in appearance and deportment, the speaker was a girl of twenty. She had long red hair, bound back by a blue silk band to form what a later generation would call a "pony tail". Her face was very pretty, with a scattering of freckles and a slightly snub nose which enhanced rather than detracted from its attractive lines. There was a healthy glow to it and a suggestion of the high spirited zest for living which had caused her to leave the mansion of her family in Providence, Rhode Island, and pay a visit to the border country of Texas.

As Mavis had come to the small clearing in the woodland with the intention of first swimming and then indulging in the physical fitness exercises to which her companion had referred, she was clad simply. Beneath her plain white blouse and equally cheap brown skirt, all she had on was a well worn black leotard of the kind using during practice by female ballet dancers. Her slender, yet firm muscled arms and legs were bare and she had a pair of heelless black lightweight pumps on her feet. Apart from a gold pendant watch suspended around her neck by its slender chain, she had no other jewelry with her. There was, in fact, nothing about her—with the possible exception of the head band—to indicate she was an extremely wealthy heiress who would soon be coming into control of a further considerable fortune.

"Well, that's as maybe," the elderly black woman answered calmly, her voice showing that the sentiments which underlaid the words of the girl were mutual. Starting to hoist herself from the driver's seat of the vehicle, she elaborated, "But I'm 'satisfactured' with me as I am and, happen I did get myself to shrinking away, I'd just natural' have to take to eating more so's I'd put me back on again."

"Oh come on now," the redhead protested merrily, the prowess of her companion at the table having acquired almost legendary status among their associates. "Do you really think you could eat *more?*"

"I dunno," Hettie admitted, showing more amusement than offense at the question. "Seeing's how I ain't never tried."

"I wouldn't advise you to try while we're staying here," Mavis remarked, reaching to the fastener of the chain to her watch. "You know how badly Uncle Philo hates to spend money. Oh *bother,* this catch is stuck again!"

"Come here and let me do it for you," the old woman offered and, as the girl was walking around the Surrey, went on, "Yes, sir, considering as how he's your late daddy's brother, that Massa Handle sure is awful 'on-alike'. He sure isn't the most generous feller I've ever known, nor even *close* to being it."

"Daddy's *half*-brother," Mavis corrected, feeling snobbish as she did so and wishing she could develop a greater liking for the relative with whom she was paying the visit. It was not easy staying with him in the face of his thinly veiled resentment, despite his having invited her to come to Wet Slim and examine the branch of the family business based there. Giving a shrug, she continued, "I suppose it's only natural for him to feel a certain animosity. After all, next year I'll be old enough to come into my inheri—!"

Before she could finish the comment, the redhead became aware that she and her companion were no longer the only occupants of the hitherto unfrequented clearing! Clad in the general style of clothing Mavis had seen worn by *vaqueros* during her brief sojourn in Wet Slim, half a dozen well armed Mexicans were walking from among the trees surrounding the clearing. Apart from the one in the lead, they were a filthy and unprepossessing group. Tallest and youngest of them, well built and swarthily handsome, the exception was by far the best dressed. There was something about his expression and swaggering deportment, however, which suggested he was by no means any more savoury than the rest of them. It was rather the opposite, in fact.

While all the Mexican *vaqueros* met by Mavis had invariably treated her with a politeness and respect similar to that she had been accorded from the cowhands of Texas, who were their equivalent north of the Rio Grande, her instincts warned that the newcomers might not belong to that hard working and honest fraternity. Unless she missed her guess—and she prided herself, with justification, on possessing a sound judgement where character was concerned—they meant mischief. The fact that they had arrived on foot indicated they had approached the clearing without wishing to allow their presence to be detected, as was almost certain to have happened if they had ridden through the woodland. If they had heard of her habit of bathing in the nude and then exercising in the clearing every day, should their intention merely have been to watch, they would have remained in concealment instead of allowing themselves to be seen.

As any competent peace officer with experience of criminals on both sides of the international border could have confirmed, the assessment of the redhead with regards to the nature of the newcomers was correct. They were all known members of the gang led by Ramon Peraro, temporarily under the command of Matteo Alberto Cantrell. What was more, his appearance was not deceiving. Driven by ambition, with his goal fixed on supplanting their leader in the not too distant future, he was the most ruthless and, being more intelligent than the others, potentially dangerous of the group.

"Hey!" Hettie said worriedly, breaking into the very disturbing train of thought which the summations reached by the girl had set into motion. "What do you fellers want?"

"The *senora*, what else?" Cantrell replied in passable English, grinning evilly. "You don't think we'd want *you*, do you?"

Turning with considerably more speed than she had displayed while climbing from the Surrey, her movements hastened by an awareness of the potential danger of her situation, the big woman snatched up the twin barrelled sawed-off shotgun from the front seat. Swinging around once more, drawing back both its hammers as she was doing so, she lined it at waist height towards the men.

Despite finding themselves confronted by and looking into the yawning ten gauge muzzles of a weapon possessing a very lethal potential for threatening their existence, none of the Mexicans showed the slightest concern!

Nor did any of the six even slow down his advance!

"W—?" Hettie gasped, puzzled and not a little disconcerted by the lack of response to what she had considered would prove an effective deterrent. "Y—You fellers had best just turn around and go leave us be."

"Why not try to make us?" Cantrell challenged and lunged forward.

"Run for the trees, Mavis-gal!" the big woman yelled and jerked at the triggers one after the other.

Only dry clicks sounded as the hammers fell!

CHAPTER EIGHT

I'll Cut the Bitch's Throat

Giving a derisive bark of laughter, where most people might have been displaying gratitude for what appeared to be a *very* fortunate escape from injury if not instantaneous death, Matteo Alfredo Cantrell shot forward his hands to grasp the barrels of the sawed off shotgun. Being so taken aback and disconcerted by the inexplicable failure of the weapon, which she had been assured was loaded ready for use, Hettie Bonaparte was unable to prevent it being jerked from her grasp. Throwing it aside and leering with sadistic pleasure, the *bandido* swung a savage backhand slap to her face which sent her staggering into the side of the fringe topped Surrey.

Although Cantrell was counting upon the savage blow to quell the massive black woman and reduce her to terrified compliance with his wishes, he very soon learned he was in error with the summation!

Bending at the waist, Hettie thrust herself away from the vehicle. Once more exhibiting a speed which was surprising for one of her bulk, she launched an attack reminiscent of a billy goat protecting his flock of nannies from the attentions of a rival male. Hurtling forward, she rammed the top of her lowered head into the chest of her assailant. In addition to eliciting a startled and pain filled croak, the impact also flung him backwards to collide with and knock the two men following close behind him from their feet. They all went down in a cursing, limb flailing heap and with her descending on top of them. Hoisting up her voluminous gingham skirts to display a pair of enormous bare legs, she straddled the trio. Allowing all of her weight to rest upon them, she caught Cantrell by the throat with a pair of hands

77

possessing a strength many a man could not have equalled.

"Get going, gal!" the big woman instructed, pressing downwards with her body and tightening the grip on the neck of the *bandido*.

Mavis Dearington could undoubtedly behave in a headstrong and reckless fashion on occasion, but she was no fool. On the other hand, she possessed a strong sense of loyalty. Although she had been on the point of doing as she was told the first time she had received the advise to flee, observing the shotgun would not fire had caused her to change her mind. Until that moment, she had hoped the devastating effect caused by the weapon sending its spreading multi-ball load into the Mexicans would create sufficient havoc and confusion to allow them both to escape into the woodland. Seeing this had not happened and watching her companion being disarmed, she had no intention of fleeing.

As soon as Cantrell had delivered the blow, the redhead had known the spirited nature of the big woman too well to doubt that it would provoke an immediate retaliation. When this happened, having so great a fondness and loyalty to Hettie, she had had no intention of carrying out what would have amounted to a desertion. Watching what was happening, she had wished the response to the slap had taken some other and more suitable form.

As it was, Mavis realized, there was no chance of her companion being able to join her in flight!

At least, it would not be possible for Hettie to rise and run quickly enough to escape the attentions of the men who were unaffected by the result of her attack!

The correctness of the latter assumption was soon made apparent!

Chuckling at the discomfiture of the felled trio, the largest of the unaffected *bandidos* went quickly and effectively to their assistance. Stepping around, making no attempt to draw a weapon, he drove a kick as hard as he could into Hettie's side. A gasping cry of agony burst from her as the sharp toe of the riding boot struck home with a brutal and nauseating force against her side and broke two of her ribs. The sheer pain of it numbed her senses and rendered her helpless. Feeling the choking grasp of her fingers relaxing on his throat, Cantrell surged upwards to topple her without resistance from astride himself and the pair of cursing men struggling to escape from beneath him.

As Mavis saw the treatment to which her companion was subjected, anger drove all thought of flight from her!

And every other sensible consideration!

The yell of rage which the redhead let out was closer to animal than human!

Forgetting the lessons of basic self defense acquired during her harum-scarum tomboy childhood, when she had found the companionship and games played by boys more to her liking than those of her own sex, Mavis hurled herself bodily at the Mexican who had delivered the kick. Acting on pure, primeval instinctive guidance, she arrived with arms and legs flailing wildly. Sending the *sombrero* flying from his head until it was halted by its *barbiquejo* chinstrap, while her feet were hacking at his shins, she sank the fingers of her right hand deep into his long, lank and greasy black hair. At the same time, the left started raking at his face in a mindless reaction which—due to her always keeping the fingernails trimmed off—was neither sufficiently damaging nor painful to prove effective. In spite of that, the sheer animalistic fury of her attack forced him to stagger backwards with her clinging on and continuing the unthinking and not over productive onslaught.

"It looks like Juan Pablo isn't doing too good," remarked the shorter of the remaining pair who had avoided being felled by Hettie.

"We'd better go and rescue him, *amigo*," replied the other, also clearly finding the predicament of their companion more amusing than alarming. "Come on!"

Before the bewildered Juan Pablo could think of offering any resistance to the furious hair pulling, kicking and clawing of the redhead, the two men came to his assistance. Closing in from the rear, although it was unlikely she would have noticed them if they had approached from in front of her, they each grabbed her with both hands. Feeling herself caught by the arm and shoulder from each side and dragged backwards, she was unable to retain her hold on the *bandido*. For all that, on being hauled away, she tore out the handful of hair she was grasping. As he stumbled clear of her, bellowing in rage and pain, she gave all her attention to trying to escape from the restraint being placed upon her.

Such was the wiry strength induced by the physical exercises and healthy life Mavis led, that the violence of the vigorous resistance she was expending made her captors hard put to keep their holds on her. Its sheer fury prevented them from taking more effective means of subduing her. Nor did the sight of Cantrell rising and starting to deliver kick after kick to the head and body of her recumbent companion do anything to make her desperate struggles diminish. Instead, she tried even harder to get free so she could go to the rescue of the helpless woman.

Snarling profanities in Spanish, the man from whom the redhead had been dragged returned to the fray. However, remembering the way in which their leader expected a kidnap victim to be treated, caution tempered his anger. Knocking aside her right foot as she tried to kick him, he knotted and swung his other fist. The hard knuckles caught the side of her jaw, snapping her head over. For a moment, her vision seemed to erupt into a series of exploding brilliant lights. Then everything went blank and, although she knew nothing of it, she slumped to hang limply in the hands of the two *bandidos* who were holding her. Preparing to deliver another punch, Juan Pablo saw it would not be needed and, mindful of the way in which Don Ramon Manuel José Peraro was apt to deal with those who went against orders, he allowed the fist to drop to his side.

"Hey there, Matteo!" called the *bandido* supporting the now motionless and unresisting redhead from the left side, as he and his companion allowed her to fall to the ground. "Take it easy with the old woman!"

"Take it *easy* with her, you say?" Cantrell snarled, looking around after he had driven another vicious kick into the unmoving and unconscious body of his victim. "I'll cut the bitch's throat!"

"You do and Don Ramon will cut yours when you get

back!" Juan Pablo warned, gingerly massaging the spot from which Mavis had wrenched the hair. "You know what he said for us to do with her!"

For a moment, it seemed Cantrell would ignore the warning. Then, having no doubt his misconduct would be reported to their leader if he should cause the woman to be unable to carry out the orders he had been instructed to give her, he decided discretion was the better part of valor. Letting out a snort, he turned and went to look into the Surrey in the hope of finding something worth stealing.

"She's still alive, at least!" reported the second of the men who had dragged the redhead from Juan Pablo, having come over and examined Hettie. "But it will be a hell of a time before she'll be able to get back to Wet Slim and take word of what's happened to the girl's family."

"Don Ramon's going to be riled as all hell if she *can't* get there!" the man who had been Mavis' victim declared and, there being no love lost between himself and the younger *bandido* who had been given command of the expedition, he had a suggestion of malicious satisfaction in his voice. "It's lucky for you he gave us that letter teling what's happened and what he wants, in case she isn't going to be able to."

"You should talk about what *I've* done to *her!*" Cantrell protested, being determined to avoid having all the blame laid upon him. Having nodded to the unconscious black woman, he indicated the equally unmoving redhead and went on, "The *patron* isn't likely to give you any bonus for what you've done to her."

"She'll be all right except for a sore jaw, in a few minutes," Juan Pablo asserted. "And Don Ramon will understand when I tell him how it happened." Still fingering his head gently, he continued with something close to admiration, "That *gringo* girl's as bad a hell-cat as Florencia Cazador."

"That's for sure, *amigo*," grinned the man who had examined Hettie. "The way she jumped you put me in mind of a mother *tigrillo* protecting its cubs."[1]

---

1. "Tigrillo": *coloquial name for the ocelot*, Felis paradalis. *J. T. E.*

"She was giving you and Pepe enough trouble before I came and quietened her down," Juan Pablo answered, being on sufficiently good terms with the speaker to accept the reference to his misfortune without taking offense. "How about going to fetch the horses so we can get moving."

"There's no rush to be off," Cantrell put in, having been on the point of giving a similar instruction, but resenting what he considered an infringement of his command. "By the time the old woman's able to get back to Wet Slim, the shape she's in, we'll be back across the *Rio Bravo*. Once we're over, even if her folks are *loco* enough to try to send them after what the *patron* says in his letter, no Anglo lawmen can come after us."

"And I hope *nobody* else is *loco* enough to try it, either," Juan Pablo declared. "Because, it will be god help her if they should."

"Looks like I called it right last night, Blackie hoss!" breathed the Ysabel Kid, standing in the concealment of a clump of bushes and, although he knew the precaution was unnecessary, he was holding the head of the big white stallion. Studying how the party who were passing some fifty yards away was comprised, he went on just as quietly, "Yes, sir, I was doing good ole Don Ramon an 'unjust' and he hadn't sent them after *me*."

After having completed the loading and dispatch of the two *bandidos* he had killed (knowing that the horses would deliver both them and his message to Escopeta without needing any guidance) the young Texan had returned to the fire he had lit as a lure for his trap. He had no intention of remaining by it, but left it burning to distract anybody else who should have been sent after him. He had been sufficiently far away not to hear "Cousin Gomez" and was unaware that the delivery of the message would take place more quickly than he had anticipated.

Having ridden for a couple of hours in the direction of the secret crossing, the Kid had decided to call it a day. He was making camp in an area which satisfied his need for concealment and which would cause difficulty to anyone

trying to approach while he was sleeping when he had heard
horses moving in the distance. They had been coming from
the direction of Escopeta, which he considered was a matter
demanding investigation. Taking his Winchester Model of
1873 rifle—the rounds he had expended earlier having been
replaced prior to leaving the vicinity of the ambush—and
trusting the well trained stallion not to betray its presence
to the riders by making a noise, he had set off after them.

Employing the stalking skills of a *Pehnane* Comanche
Dog Soldier, which he had acquired during his childhood,
the black clad Texan had been able to get close enough to
the approaching party to study them without being detected.
Six in number, one of whom was leading a saddled and
riderless horse, they were all men he recognized as having
been in *Bernardo's Cantina* at Escopeta earlier in the evening. But for all their appearance, he had concluded that—
unlike the previous pair from the town—they were not
searching for him. If Ramon Peraro had sent them after him,
being aware of his reputation as a night fighter, he could
not believe they would have been traveling in such a noisy
and incautious fashion.

Waiting until the riders had passed and the sounds of
their departure had faded into the distance, with nothing to
suggest they were up to mischief as far as he was concerned,
the Kid had rejoined his horse. While he had been curious
about the reason for their journey and felt it almost certainly
boded ill for somebody, according to his code, he had not
considered it to be any of his business. If he had suspected
there might be danger to a friend or close acquaintance, he
would have followed to intervene. The only person in the
vicinity qualifying for that category was Jock McKie, re-
siding in Wet Slim. Although the town was not large, even
by the standards of the Texas border country, it was too well
populated for a mere half a dozen *bandidos* to pose any
great threat to the well-being of the elderly leatherworker.
Therefore, satisfied that Peraro had not reneged on the promise he had been given, he had felt it was only fair he should
keep out of the affair. With that in mind, he had settled
down and, using the earth as a mattress and the open sky

for a roof, as he had so often throughout his eventful young life, he had rolled himself in his blankets, then gone to sleep.

Being tired as a result of his exertions in the past twenty-four hours on top of having traveled a good distance during the past few days, the Kid had slept somewhat later than usual that morning. Rising, he had eaten a breakfast of pemmican and jerky; both of which were nourishing, long lasting and easy to carry. With this done, he had saddled the white stallion and sought for a place where he could carry out his abulutions. Finding a small stream he had washed and, using the razor sharp five inch long blade of a clasp-knife from his warbag, shaved.[2] With that task completed, he had made his way in the direction of the secret crossing. It was his intention to collect the Canada goose he had hidden prior to entering Mexico and deliver it to McKie as he had meant to do before being diverted.

Especially after the way he had worded his message, which they both knew did not restrict the threat of repercussions to Jesus *"Obispo"* Sanchez and Edmundo *"Culebra"* Perez, the Texan had not relied upon his belief that Peraro would behave in a honorable fashion. Nothing he knew had led him to assume the *bandido* leader would keep to the promise he had been given if it could be broken

---

2. *The author has a strong suspicion that the trend in most Western movies made since the mid-1960's to portray all cowhands as being long haired and filthy has not arisen from the desire of the producers to create "realism". This kind of appearance was regarded as the "in" thing by the "liberal" element who were becoming increasingly influential in the movie industry. Consequently, few clean shaven and short haired actors were available, particularly to fill "supporting" roles. Our extensive reference library does not contain a dozen photographs of cow-hands— as opposed to Army scouts, mountain-men, or gold prospectors—who had bushy hair and beards. Furthermore, our reading on the subject and conversations with some of the older members of Western Writers of America— to which organization we have the honor of belonging—have led us to assume that the term "long hair" was one of derision and opprobrium throughout the "Old West" and Prohibition eras, just as it still is today. Therefore we see nothing unusual in the Ysabel Kid washing and shaving in the morning. J. T. E.*

without the betrayal being discovered. With that point in mind, he had taken precautions against either pursuit or ambush as he was making for the Rio Grande. This reduced the speed at which he was able to travel and he was still some distance from the river when he had become aware that the party was approaching. Taking cover, he had watched them drawing nearer.

Seeing the previously unused horse was now carrying a rider, the Kid had no longer any need to wonder why the *bandidos* had been riding in the darkness!

To be fair to the young Texan, he had not envisaged the possibility of the kind of crime which he now suspected was being committed!

While the Kid was aware that kidnapping formed a substantial part of the illicit revenue for Peraro, if he had thought of the contingency which he now saw taking place, he would have dismissed it as most unlikely. Never before had anybody other than wealthy Mexicans been selected as victims. Yet the evidence of his eyes was implying that this was no longer so. Nor, in view of all he had heard about this particular kind of crime as perpetrated by the *bandidos* of Escopeta, did he believe the capture of the victim had merely come about by chance. According to the information which had come his way, every kidnapping was carefully planned and organized, and the victim was always affluent, or had sufficient rich connections to make it profitable.

Studying the slender red-haired girl slumped in the saddle of the horse being led by Matteo Cantrell, the Texan saw nothing about her attire apart from the gold pendant watch suspended around her neck to suggest she would have struck the *bandidos* as being a worthwhile candidate for kidnapping if they had come upon her accidentally. Should they merely have found her as they were passing on an ordinary looting mission, which was something Peraro did not encourage north of the Rio Grande as he was too wary to invite repercussions from the Texans, they were more likely to have raped and killed her rather than bring her back alive. What was more, the fact that they had brought along only one spare mount suggested that they had been looking for somebody specific to take back to Escopeta with them.

The fact that the girl was accompanying the *bandidos*, clearly against her will, was pretty conclusive proof that she was the person they had been seeking!

Satisfied in his own mind that the redhead was the victim of a deliberate plot, the Kid next turned his attention to what he should do!

Studying the girl and her captors, the Kid began to draw his conclusions. He derived little satisfaction, or relief, from his deductions. While the bruise on the side of her cheek suggested she had had some rough handling, she did not appear to have been hurt to the point of incapacitation. What was more, despite showing signs of being under a considerable strain, she gave no indication of anything approaching a state of mindless panic. For all that, she was far from being in a position which would permit her to take advantage of any diversion he created. Her ankles were lashed to the stirrup irons and her wrists were tied to the dinnerplate sized horn of the saddle on a horse which was of far lower quality than those ridden by her escort. The loop of a lariat encircled her waist and its other end was attached to the saddlehorn of Cantrell. Either the rest of the *bandidos* were expecting pursuit, or they took such a precaution on every occasion while making their way to Escopeta from the scene of a kidnapping. Whatever the reason, they were formed in a loose semi circle around the girl and the man leading her. Each of them had a repeating rifle of some kind resting across his knees ready to be brought into rapid use should the need arise.

Regardless of the comparative ease with which he had handled Sebastian Montalban and the Acusar brothers, the Texan knew it was practically impossible for him to be able to achieve a similar success under the present circumstances. While his presence was as unsuspected on this occasion as it had been in the clearing north of the Rio Grande, the rest of the situation was an entirely different kettle of fish. Then, he had been dealing with a trio of raw and not particularly competent youngsters. The men riding around the girl were all mature and experienced *bandidos*, possessing a fight savvy almost the equal of this own.

Even aided by his exceptional skill and the extremely high rate of fire offered by the mechanism of the Winchester he was holding, the Kid realized he could not hope to kill all six men in such rapid succession as to prevent the survivors turning upon him. Fear for his own safety would not have made him pause, however. There was the safety of the girl to consider. No matter how swiftly he fired, or who was hit, those who remained would not be thrown into a state of panic. They might flee, but were sure to kill their captive by way of reprisal before doing so.

"Take it any way you want, Blackie hoss!" the Texan whispered *sotto voce*. "Should I cut in unless the time was right, there's no way I can stop that red haired gal from winding up as dead as a six day gone, stunk-up skunk. Which wouldn't do *her* any good at all."

CHAPTER NINE

Mr. Handle Don't Need No Advice

Night had just fallen when, having passed along the main street, the Ysabel Kid brought his big white stallion—to which the application of a powder he carried for such a purpose had given the appearance of a skewball[1]—to a halt outside a fair-sized, one story, adobe building in the town of Wet Slim. Light showed through the windows and, above its open front door was a weather-warped wooden sign, the sun-cracked, faded white lettering of which announced, "JOCK McKIE, FINE LEATHERWORK". The Kid was pleased to notice that the establishment was still open and that, in all probability, the owner would still be on the premises. This would save him having to spend time seeking out his old friend and, perhaps, discussing the events of the day somewhere offering less privacy.

In spite of his summations and the *sotto voce* comment made to the horse, the young Texan had decided to follow the six Mexicans and their captive for a few miles!

As a precaution, in case he should be seen by them or some other *bandidos* who chanced to be in the vicinity, the Kid had first made some changes to the appearance of himself and his mount. After applying the black powder in irregular patches to the animal, he had changed his attire for a tartan shirt, faded blue Levi's and a garishly multicolored bandana from his warbag. As his hat was in the style which was practically *de rigueur* for every self-

---

1. A "skewbald"—also called "piebald"—horse is colored by irregular patches of black and white and a "paint" is white with any other color. J. T. E.

respecting son of the Lone Star State, he had made no alteration to its shape. Nor had he deleted any portion of his armament, knowing that if he was seen from such a close distance that it could be identified, he would be recognized anyway and have need of the weapons.

With the precautions taken, the Kid had set off after the party. At last, however, he had reluctantly conceded he was wasting time which might be employed to greater advantage in another direction. The nature of the terrain they were traversing was such that, even with his considerable ability at unseen movement, he had been unable to draw closer to the party. At no time could he reach a point from which, should an opportunity present itself, he could launch the only kind of attack offering the red haired girl a chance of survival.

When the Texan had observed that the land ahead was becoming even more open, he had decided against endangering the captive further by keeping after the party. Nor, as setting her free was clearly going to be impossible, did he consider there was any urgent need to keep up his unproductive pursuit. Knowing the way in which Don Ramon Manuel José Peraro behaved towards the victims of kidnappings, provided there was no attempt at rescue or escape and the money demanded as a ransom was forthcoming, he had no fears for her safety during the remainder of the journey to Escopeta. Her abductors would be all too aware of what would happen to them should she be molested in any way while in their hands. Furthermore, as long as the instructions which he felt sure had already been delivered to her family were carried out promptly and to the letter, he was equally confident she would not be ill-treated or abused in any way throughout her stay at *Bernardo's Cantina*.

Having reached his conclusions and being satisfied he was acting for the best, the Texan had turned back without his presence in the vicinity having been detected!

While the Kid was retracing his journey towards the border, he had given thought to the affair in which he had become involved!

It was obvious that, for the girl to have been selected as a victim of a kidnapping, she must belong to a wealthy family. Yet, from what the Texan remembered of Wet Slim, he was unable to think of anybody who would be sufficiently rich to have attracted the attention of Peraro. However, as he had not visited the town for over two years, he had realized that people qualifying for such a category could have arrived either as visitors or permanent residents without his knowledge. Should they be newcomers, whether on a permanent or temporary basis, they might not be aware of the full ramifications of the affair when they heard what had happened to the girl. Fortunately, even if they obeyed an order not to inform the local peace officer, McKie was a leading member of the community and might have been consulted by them. Should this not have happened, the Kid considered his best course was to go to the town and learn the identity of the victim from the elderly leatherworker, who was sure to know it. Then they could visit the family, give advice and, provided no other instructions had been received, he could also offer his services as an intermediary to deliver the ransom money and bring back the captive.

Being aware that he was faced with a long journey to and—should his offer be accepted—back from Wet Slim, the Texan had not pushed his horse too hard as they were making for the border. While he undoubtedly would be able to obtain relief mounts if necessary, he wanted the big stallion available for use in any emergency. Its specialized training made it invaluable under such circumstances. Alert to the possibility of being seen along the way and wanting to avoid word of his continued presence in the area from reaching Peraro, he had not reverted to his usual attire. Nor had he taken the time on reaching the Rio Grande, to remove the disguise from his mount.

Primarily, the town of Wet Slim existed to serve the needs of five ranches and various other businesses in the region surrounding it. Once, it had also been a center for a thriving group of smugglers among whom the Kid and his father had been prominent. Since the death of Big Sam Ysabel and his own retirement, in addition to the fact that the reinstatement of the Texas Rangers had produced more effective enforcement of the law than had been the case during the hated State Police of the "Reconstruction" period, smuggling had decreased and the population had lost a previously lucrative source of revenue. However, the cattle industry had brought back solvency after the period of recession resulting from the decision by Texas to support the Confederacy in the War Between The States, and the citizens had shared in the benefits to an extent which, in part, helped offset the departure of the smugglers.

While passing along the main—in fact, only—street, the remainder of the buildings being scattered and erected at whatever location the whims of the respective owners had caused to be selected, the Kid noticed the small jailhouse was in darkness. There had been a number of horses tied to the hitching rails of the River Queen Saloon and the two business premises on either side of it. Judging by the noise from inside the well lit place of entertainment, he had concluded it could be pay night for the local ranches and that the crews were in town to celebrate.

Slipping from the saddle, the Texan glanced at the sign above the doorway of his destination as he was patting the neck of the big "skewbald" stallion. A grin came to his face. While McKie undoubtedly did produce leatherwork of an excellent quality, there had been a time when his main source of income had been derived from the goods carried by the Ysabels and other smugglers.

Putting the thought from his mind, the Kid lifted the Canada goose from where he had carried it suspended on the horn of his saddle. As he had made use of the secret crossing, he had considered there was no sense in wasting the big bird which had inadvertantly caused his involvement in the kidnapping. Carrying it by grasping the legs in his left hand, he had stepped silently across the sidewalk. The habit of avoiding the making of more noise than was absolutely necessary, developed in his childhood, had become second nature and was followed without the need for conscious thought. Not for the first time, he was grateful for the trait. Halting just outside, his arrival clearly being unnoticed by those inside the building, he looked through the open door and found the sight with met his gaze to be most interesting.

Showing no sign of change since the last occasion when he and the Kid had met, Jock McKie gave the impression of being a somewhat aged, but still full of sand and grit, fighting cock. Of medium height, lean and white haired, he wore a collarless white shirt, tartan "trews" and Indian moccasins. However, the absence of his leather apron suggested he was not attending to the business of his establishment. Nor did his demeanor indicate he was enamored of the man he was facing across the counter.

"And I'm telling ye the mon's oot of his senses to even *think* about doing it!" the elderly leatherworker was saying, his lined and oak brown face as impassive as if it was carved out of the rock of the Scottish Highlands from which his forefathers had come. In spite of that, to anybody who knew him well, the absence of his normal Texas drawl indicated his temper was rising. There was a noticeable asperity in his voice as he went on, "Which I'll be telling him myself—!"

"Mr. Handle don't need no advice from you, old timer!" claimed the man responsible for the annoyance. He was dressed like a working cowhand, but the low hanging Colt Artillery Peacemaker at his right side and other signs informed anybody who knew the ways of the West that this was unlikely to be his real occupation. He had all the earmarks of a hired gun fighter and his accent suggested his origins were closer to Kansas than Texas. "So, was I you, I'd stay way out of things that don't concern you."

"You're *not* me, I thank the Good Lord above," McKie asserted, his Scottish accent so thick it could have been cut with a knife. "And I'll do and say's I please without asking the likes of you if it's all right for me to do it."

"Yeah?" the burly Kansan said, his right hand moving in the direction of the revolver in its contoured fast draw holster. "Well—!"

There was a dark clicking sound and the hard-case found himself looking into the bore of the old Colt Model of 1848

Dragoon revolver which had been scooped rapidly from its place of concealment under the counter, being cocked as it rose, by the owner of the establishment. Taking a pace backwards, he hurriedly moved his hand well clear of his own weapon. While he counted himself a better than fair hand with a gun, it was well known around Wet Slim that the elderly leatherworker "took no sass, but sassparilla" and was well able to back up any play called for in such circumstances.

"All right," the man growled, trying to bluster his way clear without letting it be obvious he was backing down. "But, afore you bill in, just bear in mind how much business Mr. Handle puts your way. You'll miss it should he get riled up and stop coming here."

"I managed without his business afore he come and likely can even though he's here," McKie answered, showing no sign of being impressed. "And, like I said, I'll do just's I see fit. Which same I aim to go and speak my piece about what he's fixing to do. Happen he doesn't like *that*, he's free to take his trade any other place around here he can find to do it—Trouble being, we both know there isn't any."

"I'll take him your word," the hard-case promised sullenly.

"The sooner the better'll suit me," the leather worker declared.

Sent to sound out the sentiments of McKie towards the plans contemplated by his employer, the man—who was currently going by the name, "Ira Jacobs"—had soon discovered they were adverse. He had not even been allowed to offer the reasons before it had become obvious the old Scot was in complete disagreement. His attempt to ensure the objections were not made publicly had only succeeded in getting up McKie's dander and he could only take the matter further in a way which, even should he survive, would do nothing to help Philo Handle with what was intended. However, precautions had been taken in case the old Scot should prove intractible. Wanting to implement them, he concluded he may as well leave without prolonging the futile discussion.

Swinging around, Jacobs was in a far from amiable frame of mind when he discovered there had been a witness to his humiliation. Studying the tall figure lounging against the jamb of the door, he drew erroneous conclusions. If the Kid had been wearing the all black clothing, he might have been more impressed. As it was, studying the old Dragoon in its low cavalry-twist draw holster—the bowie knife being concealed from his view—the inexpensive cowhand attire and the babyishly innocent lines of the Indian-dark face, he decided he was looking at somebody upon whom he could assert domination as a means of working off his anger.

"You!" the hard-case barked, starting to walk across the room.

"Me?" inquired the young Texan, with a deceptive mildness in his drawl which was a strong contrast to the hard Mid-West voice of the man coming towards him.

"Yes, you!" Jacobs confirmed. "Get down to the saloon!"

"Suppose I tell you to go right out and climb up your thumb?" the kid asked, still speaking as gently as if merely discussing some casual and unimportant topic.

"I'll be willing to bet you couldn't do it, Jacobs," McKie commented, lowering the hammer of the Dragoon and laying it on top of the counter.

Even if he had not heard the remark passed by the elderly leatherworker, the hard-case would have taken grave exception to being addressed in such a fashion by somebody who he believed to be no more than a young and unimportant cowhand. He had his reputation to consider and knew this would suffer if word went out that he had allowed such disrespectful behavior to go unpunished. Letting out a low growl, he increased the speed of his advance and once more began to move his hands towards the position of threat above the butt of the revolver.

"Here, catch!"

Speaking the two words, the Kid moved swiftly across the threshold as if intending to meet the hard-case in the middle of the room. As he was doing so, he swung and threw the Canada goose ahead of him, accompanying it with an excellent impersonation of an enraged gander gobbling while launching an attack. The sound was so life-like that, taken with the sight of the big bird rushing through the air towards him, Jacobs was too startled to react by reaching for his gun. Instead, taking a long stride to the rear involuntarily, he used both hands to knock the approaching shape aside. Even as his mind was registering that the object he touched was too stiff to be alive, he found the time had passed when he might have rectified the situation.

Having created the diversion his instincts had warned might be necessary, due to his acceptance that he was not more than adequate where the rapid drawing and firing of a handgun was concerned, the Kid had made the most of it. Twisting the palm of his right hand outwards as he was throwing the bird, he closed it around the butt of the Dragoon. Although he suspected the speed with which he twisted the weapon from its holster might have proved insufficient if things had been even, he had turned the odds in his favor by the ploy.

By the time the burly hard-case had responded without thinking, on finding himself apparently being attacked by an angry Canada goose, the Texan was holding the big Colt free of leather and ready for use.

What was more, Jacobs discovered a startling change had come over the "harmless" young cowhand he had expected to browbeat without difficulty!

Crouching slightly behind the massive old revolver, there was none of the earlier aura of babyish innocence about the Kid!

Rather there was an impression of the Texan being as mean as two starving grizzly bears and just as eager for trouble!

Studying the Indian-dark face, which now bore the aspect of a *Pehnane* Comanche Dog Soldier making ready to count coup on the hated white-eye brother, Jacobs was alarmed and perturbed by the metamorphosis. He tried for a moment to meet the menacing challenge of the red hazel eyes and failed. Slowly and for the second time in only a minute or so, his right hand drifted away from the butt of the revolver towards which it had been returning. His every instinct warned that to have attempted to even touch the butt, much less essay a draw, would prove both futile and fatal.

"Hey now!" the hard-case said, in a placatory manner which was like a bitter taste in his mouth. "Take it easy, young feller, you're too quick to temper. Mr. Handle told me to collect everybody I saw and take them down to the saloon—!" Knowing his employer had become a person of importance around the town and surrounding district, he continued with the air of one who was delivering a friendly warning it would be ill-advised to ignore, "Which he won't take it kind if you don't go."

"Leave us bow our heads to Mr. Handle, *whoever* he might be," the Kid replied sardonically, showing no sign of being placated and without so much as lowering the old Dragoon. "Anyways, happen he's so all fired important hereabouts, maybe you'd best collect *yourself* and head on down there. I know the way, *should* I take the notion to drop by."

Glancing over his shoulder, Jacobs found he was being watched by McKie!

Nothing showed on the leathery face of the Scot to indicate how he regarded the situation. Despite finding it amusing, he was to wise to allow his feelings to become apparent. If he was to do so, he realized the already wounded pride of the hard-case might demand an attempt be made to recoup for the loss of face. Being aware of how competently his latest visitor could cope with such a situation, he had no doubt over the way in which such an attempt would turn out. For all that, under the circumstances, he considered the outcome would be unadvisable. With the conditions currently prevailing, the arrival of the Ysabel Kid struck him as being too providential for him to have any desire to see anything detract from its potential value.

"Tell Mr. Handle I'm coming and ask him if he'll hold off until I've talked to him," the elderly leatherworker requested, offering a way in which the confrontation could be brought to an end without hostile action by either participant. Wanting to save identifying the Kid until a more suitable moment, he went on, "And I reckon this young feller'll be willing to come along with me, after he's seen to whatever brought him in here."

"Why sure," the young Texan asserted, deducing correctly what had motivated the offer and being willing to act in accordance with the wishes of his old friend. "I'd be right obliged to go along to the saloon, only I for sure don't take kind to *nobody* telling me I have to."

Listening to the comments, Jacobs realized he was being offered what amounted to a flag of truce!

The hard-case also deduced the respective offers were not being presented out of fear of arousing his own wrath, or concern over possible repercussions from his employer. Nothing he saw about either man suggested they were in the slightest concerned over such considerations. He was all too aware that the standing in the community possessed by McKie was sufficient to counteract any threat posed by a newcomer like Philo Handle. Nor was the deadly-looking young Texan any more likely to be swayed by worries over the possible consequences of provoking his employer. While the gun still held by the "cowhand" was as out of date as that which had been produced by the owner of the leather shop, it was handled with a competence which did nothing to reduce its considerable potential. What was more, babyishly innocent as the newcomer had seemed to be on his arrival, there was nothing in his demeanor to suggest he would hesitate before employing it to good purpose should the need arise.

Accepting there was nothing constructive he could do under the circumstances, Jacobs gave a nod. Then, making sure he kept his right hand well clear of the Peacemaker, he walked by the young Texan and from the building without so much as a glance behind him.

CHAPTER TEN

Let Them Fight It Out

"What a pretty watch, *muchacha*," Florencia Cazador remarked, in the heavily accented English she had picked up during her childhood around the small towns on both sides of the Rio Grande. Strolling with sensuous grace across the luxurious second bedroom of Don Ramon Manuel Jose Peraro's living quarters above *Bernardo's Cantina,* she reached with her left hand to take hold of the item to which she was referring and went on, "*Si,* it's *real* pretty."

"It is," Mavis Dearington replied stiffly, pulling back a trifle without offering to rise from the comfortable bed on which she was sitting. "My parents gave it to me the Christmas before they died."

No snob, the slender red headed American girl was nevertheless far from enamored of the way in which the voluptuous Mexican beauty was behaving!

However, because of the manner in which she had been treated by her captors—after the first rough handling—Mavis was more annoyed than disturbed by the derisive and offensive over-familiar attitude of Florencia.

Taking everything into consideration, apart from her deep concern for the welfare of Hettie Bonaparte, the redhead was far less perturbed by her situation than she would have envisaged or believed possible if she had merely been imagining what it would be like to be the victim of a kidnapping by a gang of Mexican *bandidos*.

Nothing had happened as Mavis had anticipated!

On recovering from the punch delivered by Juan Pablo, the redhead had not been allowed to render any assistance whatsoever to the big black woman. Instead she had been compelled to stand and watch while Hettie was revived by having *tequila* splashed into the bleeding grazes caused by the kicks she had received from Matteo Cantrell and forced into her mouth. Regardless of the protests made by the seething girl, the woman—who was obviously suffering serious injuries—-had been loaded aboard the fringed topped Surrey. After an envelope had been stuffed into the pocket of her dress, the reins were wrapped around her barely operative hands and the horse was set moving in the direction of Wet Slim.

Not until after the vehicle and its barely conscious burden had gone from sight had Mavis given any thought to her own position!

Despite her educational standards on some subjects having been far less extensive than would be given to a later generation, the redhead was far from unaware of one danger she might be facing. In fact, she had heard that the raping of female captives was the usual habit of Mexican *bandidos*. However, while she had been prepared to defend herself with every means in her power before submitting to such a fate, the need to do so had failed to materialize. None of them had offered to molest, or even so much as touch, her. Neither had she been searched, nor was the gold pendant watch—the only item of value she had with her—taken from her.

Instead, when the horses had been collected from their place of concealment, Mavis had had the loop of a lariat passed over her shoulders, and beneath her arms. After it was drawn not too tightly around her waist, she had been told to mount the poorest of the animals. On doing so, her ankles were fastened to the stirrup irons and wrists secured to the saddlehorn. With the precautions against her escaping taken, the party had set off through the woodland. She had been led by Cantrell to a point on the Rio Grande at which she had considered a crossing would prove extremely difficult. This had not been the case. Rather she had found it was easy to go over due to some freak of geography causing the current to flow more easily and the water level to be lower than it seemed at first sight.

The journey from the river to the small town which the redhead had learned was named, "Escopeta" had passed uneventfully. By the time the journey had ended, aided by her excellent physical constitution, she had already thrown off the worst effects of the blow. However, having accepted that escape was impossible under the prevailing conditions, she had concentrated upon saving her energy and strength. As a result, even the throbbing pain had died away from her jaw.

Although Mavis had found nothing about which she might complain in her reception at *Bernardo's Catina,* she had been left with no delusions over her exact status. Introducing himself as "Don Ramon Manuel José Peraro", with an air of such pompous pride she might have found it amusing or pretentious under different circumstances, the leader of the *bandidos* had explained the situation in a way which left her in no doubt of what a potentially dangerous a predicament she was in. Genteel manners notwithstanding, she had deduced he was a ruthless man who would not hesitate to carry out the thinly veiled threats he had made when describing what would happen should the ransom he had demanded fail to be forthcoming.

Despite considering she was in no immediate danger, the sum required for her safe return being well within her own means to supply, it had been far from pleasant for the redhead to think of how much her future well being and life even was dependent upon her father's half-brother. Knowing she would not come into possession of her considerable fortune, over which Philo Handle had control, until her next birthday, she was all too aware of how much he had to gain should he refuse to pay the ransom.

Not that Mavis believed the refusal would take place!

For all that, the redhead had been unable to prevent herself from considering the possibility!

Escorted upstairs and into what Peraro had described as the "guestroom", Mavis had found it to be spotlessly clean and excellently furnished. In spite of the grim warning underlying the explanation, she had been amused by his indicating the sturdy iron bars at the window and remarking that they had been installed to remove the temptation of trying to escape from his "honored visitors". Such attempts as had been foolishly made, he had gone on, invariably ended in failure. What was more, the would-be escapers had always been caught outside the town and by men who were so annoyed by the inconvenience that they had inflicted painful summary punishment.

Having taken the warning to heart and being of a philosophical nature, the redhead had decided to avoid doing anything which might bring such percussions on her. Left alone, she had laid on the comfortable bed and fell asleep. Night was just falling when she awoke, but she had felt completely refreshed. Clearly having heard her stirring, a girl who had the appearance of being an Indian and employed in a menial position had looked into the room and announced food would be coming shortly.

However, when the door had next opened, it was not the Indian girl who came in!

Remembering the way Florencia had behaved in the barroom, Mavis had deduced something of her relationship to Peraro. While they had not spoken to one another, the redhead had found the mocking scrutiny to which she had been subjected by the Mexican beauty most irritating. Nor had the demeanor of the other been any less annoying as she had sauntered across the bedroom, flaunting a body which the redhead was willing to concede was exceptionally curvaceous.

"A present, heh?" Florencia said, her gaze filled with disdain and mockery, still fingering the watch. "Well, maybe you should give it as a present to me."

"Certainly not!" Mavis refused. "I told you who gave it t—!"

"I said I wanted it, *muchacha!*" the Mexican girl interrupted, giving a tug which snapped the chain. "And I'm taking it!"

"Give it back to me!" the redhead demanded, starting to rise.

"Like hell!" Florencia answered, placing the palm of her right hand against Mavis' face and shoving.

Caught unawares and off balance, the redhead was returned to the bed. Before she could regain her wits, the Mexican girl had tipped her on to her back and was kneeling astride her stomach. Held down by the weight, which was pressing her deep into the thick and soft feather mattress, she was unable to exert anything like the full power of which her slender body was capable. Instead, as she struggled feebly, the watch was dangled before her eyes and her left breast was siezed.

"I said I'm taking this, *muchacha!*" Florencia announced, working the fingers and thumb of her right hand as if kneading dough for making bread. Reveling in the agony she was clearly inflicting upon the weakly responding *gringo* girl, she continued in a savagely sadistic tone, "So I'm taking it and if you tell Don Ramon what I've done, I'll tear you into little pieces—Savvy?"

"G—G—Get o—off m—m—me!" Mavis croaked, trying to pull the hand from her bosom and being hindered by the depth to which she was embedded din the mattress she had earlier regarded as most comfortable.

"I said do you *savvy?*" Florencia hissed, giving a squeeze to the mound of feminine flesh she was grasping and eliciting a squeal of torment from its recipient.

"Y—Yes!" Mavis replied, in something close to a sob, the pain bringing tears to her eyes. Realizing she was merely adding to instead of reducing her suffering by pulling at the wrist she had grabbed instinctively, she released her hold and repeated, "Y—Yes. I—I un—understand!"

"*Bueno*, I thought you would!" the Mexican beauty declared and, giving a final grinding motion with her talon-like fingers and thumb, went on, "That's to make sure you don't forget what you'll get if you start whining to Don Ramon, *muchacha!*"

Uttering the reminder, Florencia opened her hand and wriggled from the bed. Standing with arms akimbo and legs spread apart, in a way which displayed her magnificent body to its best advantage, studying the expression on the face of the American girl satisfied her that she had acheived her purpose. Although the presence of *Senora* Castrillo had prevented her from carrying it out last time, on every other occasion when she had been able to deliver the warning in such a painful fashion, there was no complaint about the theft. Nor did she anticipate there would be from her most recent victim. From what she remembered of the *gringo* women she had seen during visits north of the *Rio Bravo,* (with the exception of ones who were sufficiently poor to have come from backgrounds similar to her own) they had no more aggressive spirit than the pampered *Creoles*[1] who were usually selected for kidnapping by Peraro.

Giving a disdainful laugh as she gazed into the tear filled eyes of her victim, the Mexican girl turned around. Swinging the watch by its chain, she began to stroll in an insolently hip-rolling and sensual fashion away from the bed. Her whole demeanor was indicative of the contempt she felt for a person who would allow her to take a treasured possession in such a feeble and craven fashion.

Unknowingly, Florencia was making a mistake!

Unlike the wealthy Spanish girls who had previously been the subjects for the kidnappings, most of whom were not long from a cloistered existence in mission schools, Mavis had been encouraged all her life to be sturdily independent and courageous!

Therefore, despite having been caught unawares and rendered incapable of making an adequate resistance because she had been sunk so far into the yielding and clinging mattress, the redhead did not have the kind of nature which was willing to let such treatment go unavenged!

Struggling until she was free from the clutches of the bed, Mavis came to her feet. Sucking in a deep breath, she angrily wiped away the tears with her left hand and her right gingerly massaged the throbbing breast. Then, with her vision cleared although the ache from her bosom continued, she flung herself after the departing girl. Despite her anger, she instinctively refrained from giving any verbal notification of what she was intending. Nor, muffled as they

---

1. "Creole": *used in this connotation, a person of pure Spanish origins.* J. T. E.

were by the thick carpet, did her pumps make any sound as she was advancing. Closing the distance, she attacked as directed by memories of numerous childhood scuffles.

Struck unexpectedly from behind, Florencia felt an arm pass around and tighten across her throat, while another encircled her waist. Shoved forward by the impact, the weight of her assailant was to her left. Giving a strangled screech of protest, she was dragged over sideways to land on top of her attacker. This proved to be no advantage. Before she could think of capitalizing upon her position, she was rolled over the body of the other girl and on to her stomach. The original holds upon her were released, but this was just as lacking in benefit as alighting on the redhead had been.

Given no time to think of taking any action, Florencia found herself being straddled and held down. One hand sank into her back hair, twisting at it and grinding her face into the carpet. The other set of fingers and thumb caught her just as fiercely by the left wrist. Momentarily dazed by the unexpected turn of events, despite the thickness of the floor's covering having cushioned her landing and saved her from being more adversely affected, she was unable to prevent the shaking to which the trapped limb was being subjected from causing her to release the watch she had stolen.

At which point, Mavis displayed an equally poor judgement!

Releasing the wrist and hair on seeing her property fall to the floor, the redhead compounded the folly by easing herself upwards a trifle. Relieved of the weight and grips upon her, Florencia responded immediately. Leaning and reaching towards the watch, Mavis heard a noise similar to the furious spitting of a cat confronted by a dog. Before she could comprehend what was portended by the sound, the thinly clad body underneath her thrust upward with a convulsive heave of such force she was dislodged and over balanced. Toppled from her briefly occupied perch, she rolled away from the Mexican girl.

Coming to a halt after a couple of involuntary turns, the

redhead thrust herself on to hands and knees. Not far away, she saw Florencia was doing the same. Their eyes met and, for a moment, they crouched motionless. Then, as if on the receipt of a signal, they propelled themselves at each other with all the fury of a pair of enraged bobcats contending for ownership of a choice piece of food. Coming together, hands driving ahead to respectively sink into hair or grab at flesh, the force with which they made contact almost brought them to their feet.

Not quite, however!

Still locked together, but with no conscious control over their movements, the girls tilted sideways and fell. Nor did their return to the floor cause them to break apart. Instead, to the accompaniment of angry squeals and furious exclamations in two languages, they began to roll across the carpet. They went in a whirlwind tangle of flying arms and legs, flailing hands, waving feet and snapping teeth.

Opening the door to bring in the meal she had fetched from the kitchen, the Indian girl who acted as maid to the kidnap victims stared at the embattled pair for a moment. Then, mindful of the treatment which Peraro insisted be given to such captives, she gave an alarmed squawk and dropped the tray she was carrying. Spinning around, she fled along the corridor towards the stairs leading to the first floor.

Engrossed to the exclusion of every other consideration in their wild and close to mindless struggling, neither the redhead nor the Mexican beauty realized the young woman had come and gone!

If she had seen the maid, being equally aware that her behavior went against the rules of conduct towards the victims of kidnapping laid down by the *bandido* chief, Florencia might have tried to break off the fight and flee from the *cantina* before his retribution could descend upon her!

As it was, not knowing her activities had been discovered by a person with no cause to hold friendly feelings toward her as a result of her bullying and over-bearing behavior since becoming the mistress of Peraro, the black haired beauty went on doing something which was likely to lead

106   *J. T. Edson*

to her being made to regret the greed which had led her to flout his wishes.

"Is something troubling you, Jesus?" Ramon Peraro inquired, as he stood at the counter with his two sub-leaders and the *alcalde* of Escopeta.

"Not *me, patron*," Jesus *"Obispo"* Sanchez replied, turning his gaze from where the Indian girl employed as maid for the kidnap victims was going towards the stairs with a tray of food for the latest acquisition. Nodding towards the *bandidos* who were assembled in the barroom, he went on, "But some of the men are wondering why you had the *gringo* girl brought here. You've always insisted we didn't do things like that north of the *Rio Bravo,* as it could bring us trouble."

"My boys aren't worried about it," Edmundo *"Culebra"* Perez asserted. "If those 'mother-something' *Tejanos* think they can come down here and fetch her back, we'll give them the same that *Presidente* Santa Anna gave those other bastards at the *Mission San Antonio de Valera.*"

"I don't doubt *that,*" Sanchez answered, but refrained from pointing out he shared the opinion of many other Mexicans that the loss of lives incurred during the siege of the establishment to which his rival had referred had played a major part in the defeat of *Presidente* Antonio Lopez de Santa Anna at the decisive Battle of San Jacinto on Thursday, April the 21st, 1836.[2] "But the *patron* has always steered clear of taking their women and one as rich as this will have a family with enough influence to have the Yankee Government complain to Mexico City—And *that* could bring down on us the kind of trouble we *don't* want."

Glancing from one to the other of the sub-leaders as they were speaking, Peraro was disturbed by what he had heard. It was the first time either had openly questioned a decision

---

2. *Some details of the siege of the* Mission San Antonio de Valera, *more commonly known as "the Alamo" and the Battle of San Jacinto are given in the* Ole Devil Hardin *series and* THE QUEST FOR BOWIE'S BLADE. *J. T. E.*

he had made. Yet Sanchez had just done so. Nor had there previously ever been any reference to *"my* boys", with the emphasis on the first word plainly indicating the formation of cliques within the gang as a whole.

To the *bandido* chief, the diversions from normal behavior were a cause for concern as they were tantamount to a challenge to his authority!

When they had first met their leader earlier in the day, Sanchez and Perez had been ill-at-ease. Each had expected to be taken to task, if nothing worse, for their respective and equally abortive attempts to kill the Ysabel Kid. Although inwardly seething at the need to do so, being mindful of the plans he had for the near future, Peraro had merely thanked them for trying to do him a good turn even though the double failure had cost the gang two "good" men.

Judging the conversation which had taken place, the *bandido* chief suspected he had made an error in tactics. Unless he was mistaken, the two sub-leaders regarded his acceptance of their disobedience as sign of weakness. In the kind of society he ruled, such a supposition could lead to serious trouble unless it was suppressed. Unfortunately, with the conditions he expected to prevail shortly, he was unable to carry out the suppression for the time being.

Listening to Perez declaiming there was no kind of trouble *"his* boys" could not handle, Peraro wondered what to do for the best. As yet, no warning had arrived that the events he anticipated were forthcoming. Once the information was received and passed on, both sub-leaders and their respective cliques would have plenty to occupy their attention.

What was needed, the *bandido* chief told himself mentally, was some form of diversion to keep the two factions distracted until the news he was expecting reached him!

Even as Peraro was wondering what kind of distraction he could arrange, his thoughts on the subject were diverted!

A startled feminine shriek rang out from the second floor!

"Patron! Patron!" the Indian maid yelled, dashing down the stairs. "Florencia's attacking the *gringo* girl!"

"You'd better go and stop her, Pepita!" Sanchez said to

the massive Yaqui Indian wife of the nominal owner, who always acted as pacifier if there was conflict between the women.

"Bring them down here, Pepita!" Peraro corrected, feeling that providence was playing into his hands by supplying the diversion he was seeking. "From what Juan Pablo and the others said, that *gringo* girl is pretty tough. So we'll let them fight it out and see just how tough she is."

"I don't care what Juan Pablo said!" Perez declared eagerly. "My money's going on Florencia."

Despite the challenging look directed at him by *Culebra*, Sanchez made no reply. He was far from adverse to watching the spectacle of two beautiful women fighting, but felt puzzled at being presented with the opportunity to do so. From all appearances, Peraro was condoning an attack upon a kidnap victim. Yet this went against the rules which he had laid down for how such a person must be treated and which he had always previously insisted were enforced.

CHAPTER ELEVEN

All They'll Do Is Get Her Killed

"Why howdy, you-all, Lon!" Jock McKie greeted, thrusting the Colt Model of 1848 Dragoon revolver into his waist band and starting to walk around the counter, after the unwelcome visitor had disappeared along the sidewalk. "I *never* thought I'd live to see the day I'd admit it, but right now I'm as pleased's a hound dog with two tails and his own forest to see you."

"I always affect folks that way," replied the Ysabel Kid, despite having a good idea what was the main reason for the pleasure. "But shucks, Jock, I know you're getting on long in years and aren't nowheres near so spry as back when. Only I never figured you've got so all-fired ancient and 'dee-crepit' you couldn't head out and nail a Canada honker for yourself." Strolling forward while speaking, he picked up the bird and, looking around him with what appeared to be disdain, continued, "Though I must admit truthful, you look a whole heap older and more ornery than last time I saw you. But this place hasn't changed a smidgin. I do declare you've still got all the same dust over everything."

"If the sins of fool Sassenach fathers aren't visited upon their even worse sons, there's surely no justice in heaven because they god-damned well should be!" the elderly leatherworker claimed. Then he went on in a tone which a stranger would not have realized was more serious, although his latest visitor knew this to be the case. "You couldn't've come at a better time, boy. Philo Handle's fixing to shake up some real bad trouble."

"Philo Handle?" the young Texan inquired.

"You wouldn't know him," McKie answered. "He bought up old Pan Brigg's place. Pan sat in on a poker game down to the River Queen one night and, being liquored more than somewhat, figured the two aces he'd been dealt would look a whole heap healthier should he add them to the pair he'd got tucked into the leg of his boot."

"I've heard tell of other fellers's got took with the same notion," the Kid admitted, noticing the voice of the elderly leatherworker had reverted to its normal Texas drawl now the unpleasant interview with Ira Jacobs was over. "Thing being, 'most all of them come to regret it."

"Which same happened to Pan," McKie confessed. "Although, to be fair to him, I've got to admit he was tolerable unlucky. Another gent in the game held him a pat-dealt ace high straight and, after the shooting was over, the sheriff sold off Pan's spread for back taxes. Mr. Philo Handle from back East put in the top bid and took it over. Got him some right smart notions, for a dude. Allows to clear off all those half wild longhorns's are eating out his grazing land and bring in some of them fancy whitefaced Herefords in their place."

"It'll come all through Texas, 'cording to Dusty," the Kid stated, his attitude indicating he considered the opinion of the man he named set the seal of approval on the replacement of longhorns by Herefords. "Fact being, he's already giving it a whirl back home on the OD Connected."

"Like I said, *Mr.* Handle's a right smart feller," the elderly Scot replied. "In *some* things!"

"But not in others?" queried the Kid, concluding from the continued employment of the honorific, "Mr.", that McKie did not approve of the newcomer.

"Like you say, *Cabrito,* but *not* in others."

"Such as?"

"Well now, as a f'r instance," McKie explained. "Seems like his niece, or whatever kin she be, was kidnapped by *his* friend and *his,* if nobody else's, good ole Don Ramon Manuel José Peraro."

"Except he's never done it over this side of the Rio Grande," the Kid drawled. "That's *always* been 'his friend and his', good ole Don Ramon Manuel José Peraro's way of picking up the odd *peso* or so."

"I'm not gainsaying it," the elderly leatherworker declared, studying his visitor with suspicion. "Only why do I get this strange feeling's how *you* know about it happening, *Cabrito?*"

"Well now," the Indian dark young Texan answered. "That could *just* be because I do know it's happened."

"There's some's might ask how come you got to know about it."

"There's some's'd get told it's because I saw Cantrell, Juan Pablo and four more of them taking her to Escopeta. Only there was no way I could see to cut in and pry her loose quick enough to stop her getting killed in the fussing."

"Those boys aren't yearling stock fresh set foot on the range," McKie stated. "And I'd tell the world you done right not to give it a whirl."

"*Gracias,*" the Kid drawled. "How'd they come to grab her?"

"Young Miss Mavis Dearington, her being the niece or whatever she might be, is a real nice young lady, considering she hails from Providence, Rhode Island," McKie replied. "Which it wouldn't be right 'n' proper to hold *that* against her. No more than it would be to hold it against me 'cause some of the folks I have coming in here start throwing goddamned Canada honkers at my good cash paying customers—!"

"Here!" the Kid commanded, holding out the dead bird with an expression of well simulated loathing. "Take the god-damned thing, seeing's I got into this whole blasted game on account of hunting it for you."

"For *me?*" McKie asked, looking and sounding as if the possibility had never occurred to him. Accepting the gift, he continued, "Anyways, seem's how Miss Mavis's been going along the river a ways 'most every morning since she come here, to swim and take some fancy exercises's'll help her to do that fancy ballet dancing's city folks take such a shine to."

"She go *alone?*"

"Nope. She's got this real big colored gal goes along. Right feisty lady, on all accounts. Totes a sawed-off scattergun with her and, 'cording to what I heard, she sprayed some of the Forked Stick cowhands with rock salt second day out for sneaking around, trying to watch Miss Mavis at it."

"There's some's'd say it's a right pity she didn't have it along today," the Kid remarked. "Or, happen she did, I'd allow she wasn't give' a chance to use it. None of those yahoos with the lady showed signs of being hit, even by rock salt."

"She'd got it along," the elderly leatherworker corrected grimly, placing the Canada goose on top of the counter. "Trouble being, what I heard, this time the god-damned thing didn't cut loose with *nothing* from either barrel when she tried to throw down on them with it."

"Why not?"

"She doesn't know, but reckoned she was told it was all loaded up and set to go when it was given to her this morning. And she didn't have it with her for Doc Dalrymple and me to see could we find out why it hadn't gone off."

"You and Doc?" queried the Kid. "Where-at's Abe Minsey?"

"Got word yesterday the sheriff wanted to see him urgent' over to the county seat," the Scot explained, the man in question being the local deputy sheriff who also served as town marshal. "So he's not around, more's the god-damned pity."

"Cantrell and his *amigos* sent the big colored gal in with the word, huh?" the Kid guessed, knowing something of how the kidnappings carried out by Peraro's gang were organized.

"They sent her in, the lousy sons-of-bitches!" McKie confirmed, with a wrath and vehemence which surprised his young visitor who knew his normally phlegmatic nature. "Which, the way they'd worked her over, she's got more guts than you can hang on the big corral fence to have made it here and tell what happened. Seems they loaded her in the Surrey and set her to heading here, but something spooked the hoss and she was tossed out. Doc says, way she was stove up afore that, he doesn't know how the hell she got to town as quick as she did, or at all, comes to that."

"What's happening now?" the Kid wanted to know.

"We sent word to the spread and Mr. Handle's come in," McKie obliged, his normally impassive face dour and foreboding.

"You mean *you* had to send for *him?*" the young Texan growled, being aware of the proclivity of Western trained horses to return to what they regarded as being home if finding themselves at liberty to do so.

"We had to send for him," the Scot replied, knowing what had provoked the question. "He said the Surrey hadn't got back to the spread. Only's Miss Mavis'd said she'd be staying in town all day, he hadn't thought nothing about it. Then he went to the place they have here in town to see about getting the ransom money together, or so Doc and me thought."

"Only he hadn't?" the Kid stated more than asked, not caring for the conclusions he was beginning to draw.

"He for certain sure *hadn't!*" McKie agreed. "Going by what Jacobs was saying just afore you dropped by, he's down to the River Queen now and he's figuring on raising enough men there to go pry her loose."

"Hell's fires!" the Kid ejaculated, his voice barely more than a whisper and his savage red hazel eyes boring into those of the elderly leatherworker. "You *can't* mean's how he's figuring on going down to Escopeta with a bunch of *hombres* and try to haul her out at gun point?"

"That's what he's figuring on!" the Scot answered.

"The god-damned fool!" the young Texan spat out. "All they'll do is get her killed. Doesn't he know the way Peraro handles kidnappings?"

"He *can't* know!" McKie claimed. "Or, happen he *has* heard, he's for certain sure not taking it to heart. Only me, I can't see him *not* knowing. He's only a dude not long in Texas his-self and I don't reckon Jacobs's ever been south of Kansas afore arriving with him, but he's got some jaspers riding for him who ought to be able to tell him what'll happen to Miss Mavis should they go after her."

"Then why's he so all-fired set on going?" the Kid wanted to know.

"Jacobs didn't say," McKie answered. "Only, from what I've seen of him, Handle's the kind who just *won't* listen to anything the hired help tells him."

"Which it's right lucky *I'm* not hired by him!" the Kid asserted savagely. "Because he's sure's shit going to listen to *me!*"

Watched by the highly amused occupants of the barroom at *Bernardo's Cantina,* the enormous Yaqui Indian wife of the nominal owner was half carrying, half dragging Mavis Dearington and Florencia Cazador down the stairs from the second floor.

As was the case with Hettie Bonaparte, Pepita possessed a remarkable turn of speed for one who was built on far from sylph-like lines. What was more, in addition to being fast on her feet, she had strength which would have put many a man to shame and was experienced in quelling physical conflict between other women.

Arriving at the bedroom, the big woman had found the girls engaged in a hair tearing struggle on their feet. Going over and grabbing each by the scruff of the neck, she had jerked them apart. However, being mindful of the instructions she had received from Don Ramon Manuel José Peraro, she had modified her usual technique for coping with such a situation. Instead of banging their heads together to stun them both,[1] she had held them at arms' length and, ignoring their furious attempts to escape her grips, hauled them bodily along the corridor to the top of the stairs. Although neither was a weakling and each was struggling wildly, they were unable to escape from her grasp.

Reaching the ground floor with her double burden, Pepita gave a shove which sent Mavis staggering into the center

---

1. *A similar technique was employed during the Prohibition era by Minnie Lassiter, "madam" of the Premier Chicken Ranch, El Paso, Texas, to end fights between her "girls", see:* RAPIDO CLINT. *J. T. E.*

of the barroom. It was unlikely that any friends of the redhead would have recognized her at that moment. All her veneer of well bred culture and civilization was gone, leaving a furiously primeval being. The silk band had gone from her hair, which was no longer neat and tidy. Torn away from the left side, her blouse flapped half on and half off. Not that she was giving any thought to her appearance. The way in which she had been handled by the big woman had done nothing to bring her to her senses. At that moment, in fact, she was not even aware of where she was or of the audience around her.

Even if the redhead had wished to avoid continuing the fight, she would not have been presented with an opportunity. Before she had fully come to a halt, much less found out she was being watched by lascivious eyes, Florencia was propelled towards her. Already strained by the luscious body inside it, the flimsy blouse worn by the Mexican beauty had been even less able than that of Mavis to withstand the stresses and strains inflicted upon it. While it still clung to her, it was torn so badly most of her torso was exposed. If she knew of this, she paid it not the slightest attention. She was, in fact, solely concerned with resuming her attack upon the hated *gringo* who had caused her considerable pain prior to their brief, forcible separation.

Seeing the dishevelled Florencia rushing at her, face distorted by rage and hands extended like the talons of an eagle reaching for its prey, the redhead plunged heedlessly into the fray. Rushing towards one another, like two trains on a collision course while using a single railroad track, they met. There was no attempt at strategy or deliberately thought out attack. Instead, locked to each other by clutching hands, they spun around with bodies twisting and turning in what seemed to be a primitive dance ritual inspired by violence and hatred. It was clear to the excited spectators that each wanted to tear the other to pieces and that they were being guided by primeval instincts in their attempts. Knees and hands jabbed or grasped at flesh. Grunts, squeals, gasps and cries which were not words punctuated their efforts. For all that, despite being locked in such savagely basic conflict, one feminine tactic was denied them. Although clawing mindlessly along with their other forms of attack, neither had nails of sufficient length to inflict damage.

Pushing Mavis backwards on to a table, causing its occupants to leave their chairs hurriedly and sending the cards and money belonging to them flying, Florencia crawled after and tried to treat her as had happened earlier. On this occasion, the redhead was not caught unawares. Nor was she being thrust into something which inhibited her movements. Shooting upwards, her hands eagerly closed upon the target which had been selected by the Mexican when she was straddled and helpless. Feeling herself assailed in a most painful manner, she made the mistake of trying to pull away. Immediately, aided by having a firm base beneath her and employing the full strength of her wiry body, the red head toppled Florencia from her. Although she attained the upper position for a moment, she was unable to keep it.

Rolling across the top of the table, still locked in a tight embrace, the weight of the girls caused its legs to collapse. As it tilted over, they slid to the floor without losing their holds. What followed their landing looked much like the convulsions of two snakes put into a pit to fight with each other.[2] Entwined by arms and legs which respectively seemed to have minds and volition of their own, the pair heaved and writhed their way across the floor. Biting, tearing, punching and gouging as they went, they gave the impression of feeding upon the fury of one another to sustain themselves against the punishment being inflicted upon them.

Both blouses soon disintegrated completely under the impulsion of clutching and tugging hands. Each girl also lost her skirt, without its removal having been deliberately sought after. Regardless of this leaving her stark naked, Florencia battled on just as vigorously. In the respect of attire, Mavis was somewhat better off. Although the bodice of her black leotard was ripped assunder and its legs had lost their knees, what was left still clung to her hips and

2. *For a description of a snake fight for "sport", see:* THE COLT AND THE SABRE. *J. T. E.*

thighs to offer some slight form of privacy from the masculine eyes which were feeding on the sight.

How it happened, not even the spectators could say, but the embattled pair made their feet and stumbled apart. Not so that either could take flight, however. Instead, they immediately reeled inwards filled by a mutual desire to continue the murderous fray which had left bruises, welts and teeth marks on each sweat-soaked body. Oblivious of the perspiration which diluted the blood each was shedding from her nostrils, they had only one thought between them. To fight until victorious, no matter how great the cost in suffering.

Spinning her magnificent body in a sweeping motion, Florencia sent her right foot into Mavis's belly. Although the kick had been delivered a fraction too early and was almost out of range, it arrived with sufficient force to make the redhead double over. Croaking what could have been an exclamation of delight, the Mexican staggered closer and drove up her left knee. Missing its intended target, it impacted against Mavis's shoulder instead of the temple. Nevertheless, her slender body was sent reeling out of control. Stumbling and groggy, she instinctively remained in the crouch and with her arms covering her face. Again Florencia kicked, but with far less vigor than she would have been capable earlier. For all that, the result was not to be despised. Passing between the other girl's spread apart elbows, the foot made its contact with her already throbbing bosom. Giving a cry of agony, she stumbled back a couple of steps and crumpled to her knees.

Following her opponent, the Mexican girl was so confident of success she became incautious. Despite the pain she was suffering, desperation and a determination not to suffer defeat gave the red head the will she needed to strike back. Her effort might have been doomed to failure, for she thrust herself upwards with the left hand open in an unthinking attempt to grab Florencia by the face. Instead, the base of her cupped palm caught the Mexican beneath the chin. The effect was startling to the onlookers, as well as the recipient of the unconventional blow. Back snapped her head and her eyes went glassy as she rumbled rearwards on legs which seemed close to buckling under her weight. In spite of that, she remained on her feet.

For a few seconds, the girls remained where they were!

Still kneeling, Mavis was keening softly in pain!

A similar sound was leaving Florencia as she braced herself on spread apart feet!

Silence fell over the spectators as they watched and wondered how much longer the embattled pair could last without collapsing!

If at all!

The Mexican girl moved first!

Stepping on legs spraddled to keep her upright, Florencia began to approach the crouching redhead. Knowing only a blind desire to survive and avert punishment, Mavis responded in a most effective fashion. Diving forward before the searching hands of her antagonist could reach her, she rammed her shoulder into the other's midsection. Breath whooshed from the dishevelled and tormented Mexican as she was driven backwards and they both crashed to the floor.

This time, the redhead was on top and made the most of it. Crouching astride the torso of the Mexican girl, she sank her fingers into the tangled and sweat soaked hair. While Florencia was writhing and struggling with urgent desperation, her efforts lacked their earlier force. Having had what she believed to be victory snatched from her grasp, her nerve had gone and she was feebly trying to escape. She could neither dislodge her captor, nor fend off what she knew was coming. Even as her hands were grabbing at the bosom of the American girl, her head was raised and slammed back on to the floor. For a moment, while her senses were reeling, she scrabbled feebly at the breasts. Up and down jerked her head, with another solid impact against the hard boards. She went limp and did not feel the third bang delivered by her opponent.

"Go and stop her, Pepita, it's over!" Peraro ordered, seeing by the flaccid way Florencia hung in the hands of the redhead that there would be no more fighting. As the big woman went to obey, he looked at the three men around him and announced, "By the Holy Mother, Juan Pablo was right about that *gringo*. She is a hell-cat!"

"Si, *patron*," Jesus *"Obispo"* Sanchez agreed, his face also wet with perspiration. "But what will her family say when you send her back the way she is?"

"Huh?" the *bandido* chief grunted, staring at the taller sub-leader with an air suggestive of a lack of comprehension. Then, making a visible effort to think about what had been said, he made what was an equally clear spur-of-the-moment reply, "They'll be so pleased to get her back, they'll not mind if she goes to them with a few bruises and scratches."

CHAPTER TWELVE

That's *Exactly* What it Means

"And that is how I see the situation, gentlemen. Those god-damned *bandidos* from Escopeta have kidnapped my niece, who you all know and *admire*. They've taken this beautiful young *white* lady of delicate raising and breeding to their filthy, criminal-infested town and almost killed her maid before sending Hettie to me with a note demanding ten thousand dollars as ransom. Now I'm ready to pay the money. In fact, it is here in this sack if anybody wishes to count it. I can assure you, the money means absolutely *nothing* to me where the safety of my niece is concerned. However, I feel—and I'm sure every one of you will agree—it will be creating a most *dangerous* precedents for me to pay them."

Having left the leather shop by its rear entrance, the Ysabel Kid had accompanied its owner in search of support for their intention to prevent any attempt being launched to rescue Mavis Dearington by force. On reaching the home of Doctor Augustus Dalrymple, a man much liked and respected in the area, they had been told by his housekeeper that he had been called away a short while earlier to attend a pregnancy some distance from Wet Slim. Knowing nobody else who was held in a similar high regard who could help them, they had made their way to the River Queen Saloon.

Halting outside the place of entertainment, with Jock McKie coming to a stop at his side, the young Texan listened to the speaker while looking over the batwing doors of the barroom. Wise beyond his years in the ways of the land, he liked nothing of what he was hearing and seeing. For one thing, apart from the words of the speaker—whose impassioned voice had the carrying clarity of a professional politician long used to addressing, reaching and swaying to his will every member of a crowd—there was not a sound.

Such a lack of noise had not been in evidence when the Kid had ridden by the saloon earlier!

Silence from the kind of men who formed the majority of the customers in the barroom was ever an ominous sign!

As the well filled hitching rails outside the building and its neighbors had suggested, the crews of the local ranches were out in force that night. Cowhands who rode the rugged terrain along that section of the border country being particularly noted for their hardness and salty toughness, they were a well armed and far from gentle-looking crowd. Yet, as the Kid was all too aware, they possessed the same qualities which were characteristic of all their hard-working, harder-playing fraternity throughout Texas. With few exceptions, they were courageous, loyal to the brand for which they rode, given to great generosity if faced with what they considered to be a worthwhile needy case and, especially where a "good" woman was concerned, chivalrous.

However, as was a trait of all their kind, the cowhands in the barroom could easily be swayed in the wrong direction by their emotions. Subjected to the right—or, depending upon one's point of view, wrong—form of inducement, they could be persuaded to perform acts which were ill-advised and, when considered later in a more sober frame of mind, liable to cause them grave misgivings and regrets. If they were led to believe a cause was just, while basically honest, they could even be persuaded to break the law regardless of the penalties which might incur.

Listening to and studying the speaker, the Kid concluded he had the personality and ability to play upon the less desirable character traits of the men in the audience. Despite the adverse opinion expressed by the elderly leatherworker, Philo Handle conveyed a suggestion of bluff and hearty camaraderie, held in check at that time by grave concern for the welfare of his kidnapped niece, which would appeal to the cowhands.

Ruddy of complexion, tall and bulky in build, with silver

grey hair, Philo Handle was in his late forties. While his accent was that of a well educated New Englander, he wore the style of clothing favored by such wealthy Southern owners of cotton plantations as were still being operated along the banks of the Mississippi River. There was no sign of him being armed, but McKie claimed he carried a short barreled British-made Webley Royal Irish Constabulary revolver in a spring-retention shoulder holster and had proved to be a good shot with it even if his draw was not up to the standards an expert gun fighter could achieve.

Although the young Texan was not unmindful that his outlook might have been influenced by the detrimental point of view expressed by his companion, the company Handle was keeping while occupying the small bandstand the better to address the other occupants of the room precluded him from revising his own opinion for something more favorable.

Ira Jacobs was standing at the right side of the rancher, his bearing suggesting he would take offence should there be any objections to what was being said!

To the left of Handle was a shorter, lean and rat-faced man whose Colt was tied low and who wore range clothes of the fashion dictated by local conditions. Not that the Kid considered he would ever require the garments for the work of handling cattle in the thorn-bush country of the region. He was, the young Texan knew, a border hard-case of the worst kind. A man who, in the years when the Ysabel family had run contraband across the Rio Grande, neither they nor any other honest smuggler would have considered hiring. For all that, he would have sufficient awareness of the situation to be able to warn his employer how Don Ramon Manuel José Peraro would react to any attempt to rescue the victim of a kidnapping.

Yet, if such information had been supplied, the rancher was obviously disinclined to act in a sensible fashion upon it!

"Hey, Mr. Handle, sir!" called one of the crowd, whose appearance led the Kid to assume he was more likely to be a hired hard-case than an ordinary working cowhand in spite of his polite mode of address.

"Yes, sir?" asked the rancher.

"Thishere 'pre—seed—'," the man went on, "or whatever you call her—?"

"You mean 'precedent'?" Handle inquired.

"That's the son-of-a-bitch," the man agreed. "Do that mean's how having you pay off could make Peraro and his greasers allow they can grab off other white g—*ladies* any time they've a mind to get more money?"

"That's *exactly* what it means!" the rancher confirmed. "And, while I'm *willing* to ransom my niece, I feel it is my bounden duty to consider all the other *ladies* in this area. Am I, I ask myself, gentlemen, justified in placing *them* in a position of jeopardy to save my niece by *purchasing* her freedom?" He paused as if wishing to let his audience consider the implication of what he had said, then continued when there was no response, "Or should I not be advised to call upon every man of *spirit* to go with me to Escopeta and rescue her, teaching Peraro and his *bandido* scum such a lesson they will never again dare come north of the Rio Grande and lay their filthy hands upon another white, *American*, lady?"

A thunderous roar expressing approval of the suggestion to oppose the ransom arose as Handle stopped speaking!

The majority of the cowhands in the barroom had friends among the local *Chicano* population and acquaintances among the *vaqueros* of the *haciendas* in the area across the river. For all that, there was always the underlying hostility which native-born Texans felt towards Mexicans. It stemmed from the animosity born of stories of the oppressions suffered by the "Anglo" colonists invited to settle and form a buffer state against the hostile Indians.[1] Nor had the situation

---

[1]. *The most serious grievance of the "Texicans"—as the "Anglo" colonists of what was then a part of the Territory of Coahuila were known—was that they were subject to taxation without being allowed political representation. As had happened in 1776, when a similar state of affairs had existed between the citizens of the country and Great—as it was then—Britain and which led to the formation of the United States of America, the settlers had risen in revolt. J. T. E.*

been improved by the atrocities inflicted on the orders of *Presidente* Antonio Lopez de Santa Anna after the Texicans had finally been driven to seek independence from his dictatorial rule.[2] Glancing around, the Kid sought for anybody who might back him if he raised an argument against the proposed rescue attempt. With the exception of McKie and himself, he could see only four men who were showing no eagerness to accept the suggestion of the rancher. All were seated around one table and, as well as being somewhat older, were slightly better dressed that the rest of the cowhands. Two he knew were the *segundos* of the local ranches and he guessed that the other pair was employed in a similar capacity. Yet, despite being faced with the possibility of losing the services of every member of their respective crews who were present—some permanently, in all probability, as the raid would be vigorously opposed by skilled fighting men—not one of the quartet was offering to intervene.[3]

"Let's go in and—!" McKie began, *sotto voce*.

"No, Jock!" the young Texan replied, no louder, yet with an urgency which brought the attention of the elderly leatherworker to him. "Lord, how I wish Dusty or Mark was here. Coming from us, *talking* won't stop it, way he's gotten hold of them. Let's head back to your place and figure what we *can* do to make them quit."

Even if the support of the four *segundos* could be obtained, the Kid could foresee there would still be great difficulty in dissuading the cowhands. It was obvious they had made up their minds that what they were being asked to embark upon was a noble and justifiable expedition

2. *Information regarding one atrocity, the massacre of over four hundred prisoners at Goliad, is given in:* GET URREA. *J. T. E.*

3. *The Ysabel Kid discovered later that the segundos of the four ranches had tried to warn Philo Handle of the dangers and, employing similar arguments to those he had intended to use, had suggested the ransom should be paid. They were countered by such apparent logic that, gauging the reception it was receiving elsewhere, they had concluded they would only lose the respect of their respective crews if they were to persist with their objections. Therefore, they had desisted and were hoping to exert their authority at a more propitious moment. J. T. E.*

which had the added advantage of providing a welcome break from the drudgery of their normal working lives. While they might have been willing to listen to a contrary point of view if it was expressed by Dusty Fog or Mark Counter, each an acknowledged and highly respected member of their trade, the Kid was aware that—although he would not have employed the exact words—he would lack such a rapport.

What was more, the young Texan suspected Handle was so determined to carry out the proposed rescue that steps had been taken in the barroom to silence any opposition which appeared likely to be effective. Considering by whom it had been made, the question about the meaning of the word, "precedent", was put in such a fashion he believed it had been pre-arranged to strengthen the argument in favor of making the raid. There were, he had also noticed, other obvious hard-cases—half a dozen of whom were close to the quartet of *segundos* and whose aid might be forthcoming if he stated his objections—positioned at strategic points among the crowd.

For all his undoubted courage and fighting ability, the Kid was far from being reckless or foolhardy. Such went against his upbringing. Except when having elected to carry a war lance into battle, or riding *pukutsi*—each of which was a "medicine" condition and subject to vastly different behavior[4]—a Comanche warrior took only calculated risks. He was aware that any intervention on the part of himself or McKie would be resisted. With the mood the crowd was in, even if he was to overcome his assailants, the sympathy would all be directed to them. Under such circumstances, it was most unlikely the cowhands would be willing to listen to anything he had to say.

Sharing the belief that there was nothing either of them could do verbally to dissuade the rescue bid and guessing why the Kid had expressed a wish to have one or the other of his well known *amigos* available, McKie accompanied

---

4. An explanation of what was entailed by a Comanche warrior electing to carry a war lance into battle and of the term "ride pukutsi" is given in: SIDEWINDER. J. T. E.

him. They left without their presence having been noticed by the men inside the saloon or the watchers who were keeping the leatherworker's shop under observation. As they went, they discussed the situation. Learning there did not appear to be any justification for the suspicions he expressed, the younger Texan proposed another theory which his companion admitted could be correct. Then he put forward a plan. It was anything but a sinecure, but he stated that he could think of no other way which might offer the girl an even slender chance of survival.

"You could be right on it, boy," the elderly leatherworker admitted, after a few seconds thought. "Only, should you be right on either count about Handle, do you reckon he'll be willing to go along with letting you do it?"

"Could be he won't have any other choice," the young Texan answered. "I ain't never yet seen a cowhand who'd *walk* further than from one bar to another and not even *then* happen he could ride. Which, should those jaspers in there just happen to find themselves left afoot, I reckon they'd think more than twice afore they'd be ready to go traipsing down to Escopeta town."

"You mean we're going to run off all their horses?" McKie breathed. "God damn it, boy, that'll get them riled worse'n a stick-teased diamondback."

"Which same's why it's not *us* who'll be doing it, only me," the Kid corrected. "Fact being, seeing's how you'll be down there in the barroom when it happens, I don't reckon anybody'll even think of blaming *you* for it."

"They'll sure's shit be wanting *your* hide, though," McKie warned. "And not even riding for the OD Connected'll stop 'em trying to take it."

"Likely," conceded the young Texan. "Only I don't aim to be around for them to tell me about it."

"Where'll you be?"

"Down to Escopeta, or headed there. Where else?"

"Like you say, where else," the elderly leatherworker drawled and, although he felt sure his companion had not overlooked such a potential snag to his scheme—whatever it might be—he continued, "Leave us not forget those two knobheads's Jacobs has watching my place to stop me billing in down here."

"I reckon I'll just have to stop them billing in with me," the Kid answered.

"It's your fool neck," McKie sniffed, despite having complete confidence in his young companion's ability to prevent any intervention from that source. "Is there anything I can do for you?"

"Get me the loan of a couple of good hosses," the Kid requested. "And, happen you've such lying around, I could sure use a pair of old and worn out moccasins."

"You've got 'em all," McKie promised. "Only just what have you got in mind?"

"You know how Peraro's got to be paid off on time, or she's dead," the Kid concluded his explanation. "Which being, we've got to stop that fool bunch trying to haul her out at gun point first thing. Should I pull that off, well I don't reckon *anybody* can get to Escopeta ahead of me and I'll be able to do what I'm figuring on. After I'm well clear, get hold of those four *segundos* and anybody else you *know* you can trust. Tell them who I am and what I'm figuring on doing."

"That I will," McKie promised sombrely.

If any other man had put forth the proposal he had just heard, knowing the enormity of the task, the elderly leatherworker would have rejected it with scorn. For all that—desperate and dangerous though the plan might be— he considered if there was anybody who could pull it off, the Ysabel Kid was the man who could do it.

"God damn it, Jug!" protested the bristle jawed hard-case, peering out of the alley at the still illuminated front windows of Jock McKie's place of business. "The old bastard ain't going to go down to the saloon."

"Maybe not," replied the second of the watchers. "But Jacobs told us to stay put and make sure he don't. Which *I'm* not figuring on doing nothing different."

After something over half an hour of unproductive sur-veillance, neither man was performing his duties with anything like enthusiasm. Yet, even if they had been, it was most unlikely—due to them giving their full attention to the building they were ordered to watch—they would have detected the menace which was stalking them from the rear.

Returning by much the same route they had used to reach the River Queen Saloon, the Ysabel Kid and the elderly leatherworker had continued to avoid being located by the pair of watchers. On entering through the rear door by which they had left, they wasted no time in making preparations for what lay ahead.

Having collected the ancient and worn-out pair of moccasins which had been requested, adding to them a heavy riding quirt he had claimed might be of use, McKie had gone to the small stable at the rear of his property. He owned two horses which would meet the needs of the young Texan. While he was saddling them, the Kid left by the front door and, mounting the big "skewball" stallion, rode off as if meaning to leave town. Circling when satisfied it could be done without arousing suspicion, he rejoined his host. Stripping to just his breechclout and weapon belt, he produced and donned a much more serviceable pair of moccasins from his warbag. As he intended to travel light and fast, he left his bedroll in the care of McKie. Making a bundle of his all black clothing, as he considered the need for the disguise was over, he fastened it to the cantle of his own mount's saddle and the reins of one horse to the horn.

With all made as ready as possible, the Kid and the elderly Scot separated. While McKie set off behind the buildings of main street in the direction of the saloon, the young Texan rode one horse and allowed Blackie to follow him loose, leading the other. Satisfied there would be no difficulty from allowing this to be done, he left his stallion and its companion by an empty house on the edge of town. Adding the quirt to his armament, but leaving the Winchester Model of 1873 rifle in its saddleboot, he set off to remove what could offer an impediment to the carrying out of the first part of his scheme.

Ground hitching the horse a short distance from the alley where the two hard-cases were lurking, the Kid made his approach with the kind of stealth which had saved his life on numerous occasions in the past. Knowing the kind of men they were, he felt sure they would not have listened to an explanation of his intentions. Therefore he had decided upon his most suitable line of action, although he would have hesitated before taking it if they had been merely honest if misguided cowhands. Each was wearing a hat, the crown of which would offer at least a measure of protection for the head. Knowing how much depended upon silencing both, before either could raise an outcry, he did not launch his attack in that direction.

Gripping the leather wrapped, lead loaded handle of the quirt in his right hand, the Kid rammed the round knob at the bottom into the kidney region of the first speaker. Assailed by such agony it numbed his mind and prevented him giving more than a croak of great suffering, he collapsed to his knees.

Letting out a startled exclamation, Jug spun around with his right hand reaching for the gun he wore. Unwittingly, he was playing into the hands of the attacker. Having allowed the handle of the quirt to slip through his fingers so he now grasped it by the other end, the Kid swung it in an upwards arc. The knob of the butt struck the hard-case under the chin, to the accompaniment of the crack of breaking bone as the contact was made. Crumpling like a rag doll from which all the stuffing had suddenly been removed, Jug toppled backwards with his weapon still in leather. As he was going down, his companion fell back forward in a faint and, by doing so, was saved from receiving further attention at the hands of their assailant.

In one respect, the pair of hard-cases might have counted themselves fortunate!

Generally when the Kid was dressed in such a fashion, he thought and acted like the *Pehnane* Dog Soldier he had been educated to be. Which meant he felt no compunction whatsoever over having to kill anybody he considered to be an enemy of himself or his friends. Although the two men must have been aware that the only way they could carry out their orders was to attack and at least render McKie

unconscious, should he have let them see he was going to
the saloon, they were lying in wait for him. They were,
therefore, threatening his life. As far as *Cuchilo*—name
warrier of the Dog Soldier war lodge—was concerned, this
put them into the category of enemies. By which token,
serious as their respective injuries might be, each was lucky
to still be alive.

Dragging first one and then the other limp, unresisting
hard-case further into the blackness of the alley, the young
Texan gagged them with their bandanas and, using their
waist belts, fastened their wrists behind their backs. He
knew they would be unable to intervene physically without
this being done. The precaution was being taken to prevent
either recovering and raising an outcry which attracted un-
wanted attention before he had completed what he was about
to do.

With the securing accomplished, the Kid turned and strode
swiftly in the direction from which he had come!

CHAPTER THIRTEEN

That's a Comanch', That Was

Riding the borrowed horse into the alley between the next but one and next buildings to the River Queen Saloon, the Ysabel Kid left it with its reins dangling. Drawing his bowie knife, he peered cautiously around the corner. Everything he saw met with his satisfaction.

Closing a large jack-knife, Jock McKie was already approaching the front entrance to the saloon from the opposite end to the young Texan. Otherwise, the sidewalks on both sides of the street were completely deserted. As the conspirators had surmised, the noise which now reached their ears indicated that, wanting to ensure their continued support and lessen their willingness to listen to arguments against his project, Philo Handle was lavishing drinks on the local cowhands. By doing so, he was keeping everybody in the barroom.

Making the most of the opportunity with which he had been presented, the half naked Texan emerged from the alley. Striding swiftly from horse to horse at the Hitching rails, he cut the reins of each in passing. Much to his relief, despite being liberated, none of them began to move away thus, perhaps, giving premature warning of what he was doing.

"I've done them all over there," the elderly leatherworker announced, *sotto voce*, as the Kid was releasing the last animal on the side from which he was working. Pocketing the jack-knife, he went on, "Get going, boy—And good luck. May *Ka-Dih*[1] ride with you all the way!"

---

1. "Ka-Dih": *the Great Spirit, supreme deity, of the Comanche Nation.* J. T. E.

"Save some of that good-damned goose for *me*," the young Texan requested, just as quietly. "If it wasn't for him, I wouldn't be risking my fool neck this way."

Having delivered the sentiment, the Kid returned to the patiently waiting horse. Mounting, he advanced it into the center of the street. By the time he had done so, McKie had already disappeared through the front door of the barroom. Satisfied that his old friend now had an alibi, he took another glance around and felt grateful that he was still unobserved.

Despite having achieved so much of his scheme without any particular difficulty, the young Texan knew his task was still far from being a sinecure. He was all too aware of the danger if he should be caught, or even just seen, over the next minute or so. Excellent though his motives undoubtedly were, he would not be allowed to explain them. No cowhand ever took kindly to anything which would leave him afoot and would shoot immediately, without waiting to ask why it was being done.

"Lordy lord!" the Kid breathed, drawing the pair of worn out moccasins from under the back of his weapon belt and tucking them securely beneath his left armpit. "Times like *this*, a man gets to wishing he'd led a *better* life!"

With the wry comment made and the deed performed, the young Texan twisted the Colt Model of 1848 Dragoon revolver from its holster. Then, giving vent to an ear-splitting *Pehnane* Comanche war whoop which was savage enough to turn white the hair of anybody who remembered its past connotations, he gave a signal with his heels and set his mount into motion. As it was bounding forward like a well trained quarter-horse leaving the starting line in a race, he fired a shot into the air and once again the awesome battle-cry left his lips.

Startled by the commotion, the liberated horses nearest to the point from which it was originating swung away from the hitching rail. Gathering those further along as they went, they fled down the street. Allowing the moccasins to slip from beneath his armpit as he was approaching the end of the saloon, the Kid swung over to hang along the flank of his horse. By doing so, he placed its body between himself and the outraged men he felt sure would soon be appearing.

Hearing what was happening on the street caused silence to descend in the barroom!

Everybody present knew cowhands frequently let off steam by whooping and firing a gun, but they were equally aware there were times when neither should be done!

Discovering the effect which the outburst was having on the horses they had left outside, none of the customers regarded the incident as being harmless fun!

Letting out yells of furious alarm and reaching for weapons, the occupants of the barroom made hurriedly for the front door!

McKie was the first man outside!

Such was the apparent eagerness of the elderly leather-worker to avenge the loss of the animals, he sprang into the line of fire between the men following him and the object of their outraged attentions. His old Dragoon bellowed, but without the shot taking effect. Before any of the others could get by and line a weapon, the half-naked figure hoisted himself back on to the saddle of his swiftly moving horse and followed their mounts into the darkness. As he disappeared, yet another of the savagely menacing yells left him.

"That's a Comanch', that~was, gents!" McKie announced, returning the old Colt to the holster of the gunbelt he had donned as part of the preparations made to implement the Kid's scheme. "Or I've *never* heard one."

"I don't give a damn who it is!" Philo Handle replied angrily, realizing how his proposed rescue bid would be affected by the loss of the animals. "Get some horses and fetch back those he drove off, men!"

"I wouldn't even *try*, was I you," the elderly leather-worker warned, pointing to the two objects lying in the center of the street. "'Cause he's left his old moccasins behind!"

"What if he has?" Handle demanded.

"When a Comanch' does that, it means he's 'raided'—which's what they call *stealing*—a bunch of hosses and figures he won't need to walk no more," McKie explained, concluding the rancher was too concerned over the loss to wonder how he had reached the saloon in spite of the two hard-cases sent to prevent him from doing so. "Which being, he for sure isn't about to let *nobody* take them back from him. I mind one time it happened, even went along with the feller's aimed to get their hosses back."

"What happened, Jock?" inquired the oldest of the four ranch *segundos,* studying the elderly leatherworker with a somewhat speculative gaze which was mirrored by his companions.

"We got to figuring it wasn't worthwhile going on after he'd put three of us down with a buffalo gun from way out of range of our rifles," McKie replied, delighted by the way in which everybody was listening to him. "All except one of us, that is. He'd got him a real stubborn streak and would keep going. Couple of days later, a Company of Rangers come on him. He was dead and, from the look of him, he hadn't died quick nor happy. And that, gents, is what happens should you go after a Comanch' when he's left his old moccasins on the trail."

"I don't give a damn what happened to him, or what's been left behind!" Handle stated, glaring at the elderly leatherworker. Then a realization came and he darted a glance along the street. However, putting the thought from his mind, he went on, "Come down to the livery barn with me, some of you men. I'll hire every horse there, so you can go after those you've lost."

"Yeah, come on!" Ira Jacobs supported. "No god-damned Injun's going to run off my hoss and live to ride it!"

"It's been more than a fair spell since we've had any Comanch' down this way," the spokesman for the *segundos* commented, watching the rancher and the hard-case leading away everybody except himself, his companions and the elderly Scot. "Fact being, way I've heard it, they're all living on the reservation now."

"Could be some young buck's got tired of living there and wants to try some of the old ways," McKie offered with disarming innocence. "I've heard tell of such happening now and then."

"And me," conceded the spokesman, who had played poker sufficient times with the leatherworker to believe there was far more to the suggestion than appeared on the surface.

"Only we're a hell of a way from the nearest reservation."

"There's some's might say it's *real* lucky one got took with the notion and come down here *tonight* of all nights to do some of his 'raiding', though," remarked the *segundo* of the Forked Stick ranch, another frequent participator in poker games with McKie as one of the opponents. "Do you know what that god-damned, fancy-talking dude's fixing to do, Jock?"

"I got told something about it, Sammywell," the Scot admitted, refraining from showing he heard a shrill whistle from somewhere on the outskirts of the town although he knew what it portended. "And I float my stick along with you boys in reckoning he'd've done a heap more harm than good by it."

Having no desire to put the local cowhands to too much inconvenience, or to cause the loss of the saddles which would in all probability be the personal property of each, even though their mounts might belong to the respective ranchers by whom they were hired, the Ysabel Kid had only driven the horses liberated outside the saloon as far as the edge of Wet Slim. Swinging his borrowed mount aside shortly after passing the last building of the street, he had ridden in a half-circle around the town. There had been no need for him to take the chance of being seen by going closer. The whistle which the elderly leatherworker had just heard was a signal to his big "skewbald" stallion. It would instruct Blackie to go and join him, leading the second of the animals with which he had been supplied.

When discussing the plan for disrupting the rescue bid, knowing range bred horses, the young Texan and McKie had been certain that almost all of those driven off would be retrieved without too much difficulty. Some would halt before going too far and might even return to the town. The rest would in all probability go straight back to the areas which they regarded as home.[2] On the other hand, if any

---

2. *The suppositions of the Ysabel Kid and Jock McKie subsequently proved valid. Only two of the horses, each belonging to a hard-case hired by Philo Handle, were not recovered over the next couple of days. One of the missing animals arrived a month later at the ranch from which it had been stolen, but the other was never seen again. J. T. E.*

of them should be lost, the conspirators were satisfied the Kid was acting for the best. Verbal dissuasion would not have prevented Philo Handle from leading the ill-advised expedition. Therefore, in their opinion, the means employed were fully justified if it caused a postponement of what they knew was practically certain to lead to the death and not the liberation of the kidnapped girl.

"That's for sure!" the spokesman for the quartet growled and the other three rumbled grim concurrence, but none of them gave any indication of having heard and attached any significance to the whistle. "They'd've never got close enough afore they were seen coming to get her out of Escopeta alive."

"Only, with his army being left afoot like it is," McKie commented, in such an unemotional tone he might have been making no more than desultory conversation rather than discussing a subject upon which the life of a beautiful young woman depended. "I don't reckon's how he'll be doing it tonight and who knows what tomorrow'll bring to make him call it off for good?"

"I wouldn't want to sound all suspicious, Jock," the spokesman asserted. "But how come I keep getting this sneaking feeling you're nowheres near's surprised by this Comanch' showing up 's some might reckon you should be?"

"My mama allus told me's, being the seventh son of a seventh son, I'd got what she called 'second sight'," the elderly leatherworker answered blandly. "Which same mean's I can sometimes see thing's hasn't yet happened. Like right now. I've got this feeling how your hosses might be easier to get back 'n' I let on just now."

"You mean's that Comanch's left his old moccasins on the trail just might not've been a Comanch' after all?" Samuel Barraclough hinted, beating his companions to the question.

"Like I said, I've got this *feeling*," McKie replied. "Only, right now, maybe you boys'd best be getting down to the livery barn your own selves. When those hands of your'n find there's not anywheres near enough saddle-hosses to go 'round, could be there'll be some argument over who gets what."

"Why sure," grinned one of the *segundos* who had so far remained silent. "And I'd surely not be wanting for us Box L boys to miss out on being able to go look for our hosses."

"The same goes for the Forked Stick," seconded Barraclough.

"Which same's my exact feelings on it," claimed the fourth *segundo*. "Let's go and make sure they get shared out fair. No matter how *long* doing it takes."

"After you've seen to it," the elderly leatherworker said, satisfied that he had allayed the concern felt by the quartet over the fate of the horses. "I'd be right obliged happen you'd drop by at my place to smoke a pipe, have a dram of good Scotch whiskey and jaw over old times."

"I don't know about Sam, Beau and Dirk," drawled the spokesman. "But I'd sooner hear some talk about this Comanch' who maybe isn't a Comanch' after all."

"Could be we'll talk some about *that,*" McKie admitted. "Only don't let on to *nobody* else's I'll be doing it. I don't talk too good when there's too many people listening to me."

"That *nobody* wouldn't be good old Mr. Philo Handle, by any chance?" suggested the *segundo* of the Box L. "Now would it?"

"You've guessed it as right's the Injun side of a hoss," confirmed the elderly leatherworker. "Should any of them get to know, they might get took with the notion I'm snubbing them and take their business some other place."

"We'd surely hate to have *that* happen on our account, *amigo,*" the spokesman asserted, knowing the possibility of losing such trade was not the reason for the suggestion. However, despite being consumed by curiosity, he put duty to his ranch first and continued, "Come on, boys. Let's go and stop those knobheads of our'n locking horns with each other over who-all's going to get to use the hosses first."

Leaving the four *segundos* to attend to keeping the peace between the members of their respective crews, McKie strolled along the street in the direction of his shop. Approaching the alley in which he did not doubt the two hardcases who had been watching for him would be lying incapacitated, he decided to go and find out what had happened to them. Before he could do so, he heard swiftly moving hooves. A few seconds later, he saw three horsemen galloping towards him. One he identified as the local deputy sheriff. While the others were strangers, each was displaying the silver five pointed star in a circle badge of the Texas Rangers.

"God blast you, Abe Minsey!" the elderly leatherworker growled bitterly, looking in the direction from which the whistle had originated. He realized it would be too late to recall the young Texan, who was already riding away as swiftly as only a Comanche was able. What was more, with the far from amicable mood the cowhands would be in over the scattering of their horses, it was probably unsafe for the Kid to return unless he had successfully completed his self appointed mission even with the peace officers present. Returning his gaze to the approaching riders, McKie went on, "Why the Sam Hill couldn't you and them two Rangers've gotten here half an hour sooner?"

"Mr. Handle, I'd like a word with you outside!"

Never the most amiable of men when things were not going as he required, the New Englander swung around glowering in annoyance as he heard himself being addressed in what—despite the way in which the request was worded— sounded closer to a command than a suggestion.

Regardless of his wishes, Philo Handle had made no progress in acquiring replacement mounts for the rescue attempt. The livery barn at Wet Slim held no more than half a dozen suitable animals and, such was the unanimous eagerness of the cowhands to set off after the scattered horses, there had been much heated discussion over which of them should be allowed to do so. Alarmed by the possibility of losing their personal property, particularly the saddles so vitally important in their working lives, every one of them had been determined that he should be allowed to go after the "Comanche" as soon as possible and was disinclined to chance the recovery being made by anybody else.

The arrival of the *segundos* for the four spreads had prevented an eruption of physical violence as claims were made to precedence in the hiring of the livery barn's few horses, and were countered by statements expressing a greater right to go and retrieve the stolen property. Although the cowhands had calmed down and listened to their respective leaders, without having split into opposing factions, Handle had concluded there would be a much greater delay than he had hoped would be the case before he could leave for Escopeta. Despite what he had been told by Jock McKie, he had believed a hurried pursuit of the "Comanche" would result in the return of sufficient stolen animals for his venture to be commenced.

It had become apparent from the comments of the *segundos* that they held little hope that Handle would be able to set out before the following morning at the earliest. Certainly he would be unable to depart that night as he had intended. Or, if he did, it would be without the assistance of the cowhands from the other ranches. At that moment, earlier eagerness notwithstanding, they were all more concerned by the possible loss of their property. Even his own men had similar sentiments. With the exception of himself, Jacobs and Andy Evans, they too had had their mounts outside the River Queen Saloon. What was more, unless he was misjudging them—in spite of being hired primarily as fighters rather than workers of cattle—they would refuse to accompany him unless supported by the majority of assistance which he had promised to produce for them.

Although the rancher identified two of the men who were standing at the open double doors of the livery barn, he realized neither had addressed him.

At first sight, apart from the wearing of a familiar badge of office, the speaker did not appear to be particularly imposing. No more than of middle height, in his mid-thirties, he had a sun-reddened face of almost cherubic lines and gave an impression of corpulence. A white "planter's" hat perched at the back of thinning curly brown hair. His brown

two-piece suit was rumpled and travel-stained and he had
removed the collar of his whiteshirt, while his Hersome
gaiter boots were more suitable for walking than riding. In
spite of the indication that he was a Texas Ranger, he was
not wearing a weapon of any kind in plain view.

Something over six foot tall, in his early twenties, wide
of shoulder and lean waisted, the second Texas Ranger
seemed more in keeping with the reputation earned by that
efficient law enforcement force. He had rusty red hair and
a face which, despite a badly broken nose, a scar over the
left eye-brow and a thickened left ear, was ruggedly good
looking. Dressed in the style of a working cowhand, he was
carrying in the fast draw holster of his gunbelt a Colt Civilian
Model Peacemaker with staghorn grips.[3] All in all, he was
a far more impressive figure than his companion and clearly
not a man one could cross or defy with impunity.

"Who are you?" Handle asked.

"The name's 'Anchor'," replied the man to whom the
question was directed, his Texas drawl still charged with a
polite authority which warned there was far more to him
than met the eye. "'Sergeant Brady Anchor, Company B,
Texas Rangers', in full. This-here's my nephew, Ranger
Jefferson Trade and I reckon's how you know these other
two gents?"

"I do," the New Englander affirmed, nodding with what
appeared to be cordiality to Jock McKie although the words
he directed at the stocky, middle-aged local peace officer
were more complaining than cordial. "We could have done
with you here earlier today, Deputy Minsey."

"So I hear," Deputy Sheriff Abel Minsey replied. "And
I'd've been here if I hadn't had a telegraph message saying
the sheriff wanted me over to the county seat. I met Brady
and Jeff along the way and they said the sheriff'd sent them
over to see me, which got me to thinking maybe the message
was a fake. Same being a way owlhoots sometimes use to

---

3. *At the period of this narrative, Jefferson Trade was in the process of
   changing the way by which he carried his revolver in,* THE QUEST
   FOR BOWIE'S BLADE *to that he employed in,* TWO MILES TO
   THE BORDER. *He had already bought a later model weapon. J. T. E*

get the law out of town while they do some robbing, I came straight back with them."

"Do you know who sent the fake message?" Handle inquired.

"Nope," Minsey admitted. "But it wouldn't be hard to do happen whoever did it knew sic 'em about handling wire cutters and a telegraph key."

"I suppose not," the New Englander conceded, then returned his gaze to the senior of the Texas Rangers. "What can I do for you, sergeant?"

"Like I said," Brady replied. "I want to have a talk with you and figure we can do it best outside."

"Certainly," Handle assented.

"You'd best send those boys of your'n down to the River Queen," Brady went on, as Ira Jacobs and the second man who had been on the bandstand at the saloon started to follow their employer. "We found a couple of your riders laying hog-tied and stove up some in an alley."

"Go and see to them, Mr. Jacobs!" Handle ordered, after he and the two hard-cases had swung glares filled with suspicion at the elderly leatherworker. Returning his gaze to the stocky sergeant, he went on, "Who did it?"

"The same jasper's run off the horses, likely," Brady replied blandly, giving no indication that he had been informed of by whom and why this was done. "Which it's right lucky he did it. Run off the horses, I mean, not whomped those boys of yours bowlegged. Because, Mr. Handle, happen you'd've took out after your niece, Peraro'd've known you were coming almost afore you crossed the Rio Grande. Which being, your niece would've been dead and not in a nice, quick way, even should you've been able to fight your way into Escopeta."

"Andy Evans could've told you *that*," McKie stated, nodding to the shorter of the departing hard-cases.

"He said there was that danger," Handle admitted. "But he also claimed he believed he could get us through by a way they wouldn't be watching."

"He'd've done more good happen he'd told you to pay," the elderly leatherworker growled. "He's been around the border country long enough to know Peraro would've sent Miss Mavis back safe and *pronto* as soon's the money got to him, such being his way."

"He told me that," the New Englander answered. "But he also told me what would happen to her if I didn't pay promptly, within the time stipulated and—!"

"And what?" Brady prompted as the explanation trailed to an end.

"And, gentlemen," Handle replied in a voice scarcely louder than a whisper. "As things stand, I *can't* pay him!"

CHAPTER FOURTEEN

A Throat Just Meant For Cutting

"God damn it!" Jock McKie protested, as a reduction in the volume of the conversation and other sounds inside the livery barn indicated that an acceptable division of the available horses had been reached and that saddling was being commenced. "That *isn't* what you are telling th—*us* down to the River Queen!"

"I know it wasn't," Philo Handle replied, apparently failing to attach any significance to the way in which the elderly leatherworker had amended his comment. "But I don't keep anywhere nearly so large a sum as ten thousand dollars in cash at the ranch, or in the town house either. Nor, particularly so soon after the other ranchers have drawn out the pay for their crews, does the bank here in Wet Slim hold anything like that much on the premises for me to draw and use."

"Likely," McKie said quietly, being willing to concede the point with regards to the financial reserves held by the local bank. "But why did you let on's you'd got it to hand all ready for sending down to Peraro?"

"Because of *who* I am, Mr. McKie," the rancher answered, showing no discernible objection to what might be considered unofficial questioning. "I'm a stranger here and not so well liked as I might be, which I'm willing to admit may be at least partly my own fault for bringing in my own crew." His gaze swung to the two Texas Rangers and he went on, "Without going into too many details, gentlemen, I followed advice as this is my first venture into the cattle business and the type of men I've brought with me have left my motives open to misinterpretation. You all know

143

what cowhands are like. If I'd told them the truth, they would have thought, 'That god-damned money-grabbing Yankee son-of-a-bitch is too tight fisted to hand over the cash to get his niece released.' Pretending I had it and would have been willing to hand it over, but for my misgivings in another direction, gave me what I considered to be my only chance of persuading them to help me."

"It did that for sure," McKie admitted, before any of the peace officers could speak. Aware that the kind of men brought in by the New Englander had aroused suspicion of his intentions among the other ranchers, although none of the suppositions over the reason for their employment had come to fruition, he decided Handle was equally correct in his assessment of how the local cowhands would have regarded the explanation of why the ransom could not be paid. "But surely you'd been told how dangerous it was going to be for Miss Mavis should you head down there and *try* to rescue her?"

"I'd been told," the New Englander agreed sombrely. "And, gentlemen, I assure you I did not reach my decision without much thought and soul-searching. However, remembering what happened in New York shortly before I left, I considered Mavis would be in as equally grave a danger whatever the circumstances. That is what made me resolve to make an attempt to rescue her."

"Just what was it happened in New York to make you think *that*, Mr. Handle?" inquired Sergeant Brady Anchor, having studied the speaker as well as the light allowed while the explanation was being made in a voice which throbbed with emotion.

"There was a spate of kidnappings," Handle replied. "And the victim of the first was murdered in a particularly brutal fashion because her family delayed in sending the ransom money. As I, or other members of my family seemed to be likely targets, I took great interest in their activities and hired the Pinkertons for our protection. They told me that in their opinion, which was subsequently proven correct, the first victim had been selected deliberately and had been butchered—!" A shudder accompanied the word and he continued, "Believe me, that is close to a literal description of how the young woman was killed. And it was done as an example which would frighten the families of their later victims into paying without hesitation."

Although it was difficult for the four Texans to see much of the New Englander's face, due to him standing with the light from the open door of the livery barn behind him, McKie concluded there was a vast change in his demeanor from that which had been in evidence at the River Queen Saloon. Deputy Sheriff Abel Minsey also decided he was showing none of his usual confidence and self assurance. While his expression was not discernible, his bulky frame seemed to have shrunken. All in all, he gave the impression of being under considerable strain caused by the remembrance of how the kidnapping in New York had ended in tragedy as a result of the payment not having been made as promptly as was demanded. It appeared he was so deeply concerned for the welfare of Mavis Dearington, he had been trying to take the only line of action he believed would offer her a chance of salvation.

"I reckon a thing like that'd do it for sure," Ranger Jefferson Trade remarked. "What I've heard, though, Peraro's been kidnapping folks for years now. Your niece isn't anywheres near his *first* victim."

"That may be the case," Handle countered. "But, according to Mr. Evans, she's his first victim taken from *Texas*. Isn't that so, sergeant?"

"He's never taken anybody from north of the border afore that I've heard of," Brady admitted.

"And that's why I believed it was imperative for me to make a rescue bid!" the New Englander claimed, with something close to defiance returning to his worried tone. "The time I was being allowed to send the money was so short, I suspected Peraro was hoping I wouldn't be able to deliver before it ran out. That way, he could kill my niece as a warning to the families of other victims he was meaning to take."

"So you figure he's going to take more folk from Texas?" Brady asked.

"It seems *very* likely to me," Handle replied. "There has to come a time when he runs out of victims in Mexico and needs to look elsewhere. Which only leaves north of the Rio Grande. I and my family, being newcomers and Yankees to boot, would be just what he would want for his first victims. He'd consider there'd be less risk of arousing public hostility by taking one of us than if he kidnapped—say the wife of Bilson of the Box L."

"You could be right in what you're saying," Brady claimed.

"Then you're in *agreement* with what I was hoping to do?" the New Englander stated rather than asked.

"I wouldn't go so far's to say *that*," the stocky sergeant corrected. "Fact being, happen we'd been here earlier, my nephew and I would've backed Abe in stopping you."

"Why?" Handle demanded, returning to something of his previous hardness.

"First off, to stop you getting your niece *killed*," Brady replied. "Which, no matter what you was told, there wasn't one chance in a million of *you* being able to keep *that* from happening. Secondly, should you have *tried*, there'd have been a whole heap more than just her lose their lives."

"I don't understand you!" Handle asserted.

"No matter what you was told," Brady elaborated with grim certainty. "The way Peraro'll have his scouts spread between the border and Escopeta, you couldn't've got anywheres near without him knowing you was on your way. Which being and should *you* be right about him being figuring on grabbing off more folks from up here, he'd aim at scaring off anybody else who might get taken with the notion of going to the rescue and he'd have got it set so you'd be cut to doll rags like before you came even close to your niece. If you'd come back with a quarter of your men alive, you'd be lucky." Pausing as if to make sure the full implications of what he had said would sink in, he continued, "And there's another reason why we couldn't've let you gone."

"What is it?" the New Englander wanted to know.

"Even if by some mighty slender chance you'd pulled off the rescue, there'd've been killing to do it," Brady explained. "There're politicians on both sides of the line would've called the way you did it an armed invasion of Mexican soil and they'd be ready to raise all hell over such having happened. So, being duly sworn and appointed of the law, we'd have been duty bound to stop you doing it."

"Even though refusing to let us go was going to cost my niece her life?" Handle challenged. Then he gave a shrug indicative of bitterness and resumed his less aggressive way of speaking. "Not that it matters *now*. With the horses gone and no chance of getting the ransom to Peraro on time, my niece is as good as dead already."

"Well now," McKie put in quietly. "I wouldn't go so far's to count on *that*."

"How do you mean," Handle growled, swinging in a furious fashion to glare at the elderly leatherworker. "*Count* on that?"

"Easy now," McKie requested, raising his right hand in a gesture of pacification. "No offense meant, Mr. Handle. I just said that bad. What I mean is, maybe your niece won't get hurt. Fact being, she could even be back here safe and sound tomorrow."

"She could be *what?*" the New Englander demanded, showing little sign of being mollified by the words and gesture. "I don't follow you!"

"Doc and me wondered whether you'd have so much cash on hand to pay out when we read the ransom letter Hettie Bonaparte brought in," the elderly Scot explained. "Then, when that yahoo, Jacobs, came around trying to scare me out of going to the River Queen and warning what would happen to your niece—!"

"*He* did *that?*" Handle barked. "All I said was for him to explain to you why I couldn't pay."

"That wasn't mentioned," McKie claimed truthfully.

"I'm sorry if he gave you a wrong impression, Jock," the New Englander apologized. "Mr. Jacobs is very loyal to me, but not too bright and, probably because he holds Mavis in such high regard, he may have been over zealous."

"That's how I took it," the Scot asserted, with less veracity. "Anyways, guessing how you was fixed for cash, I concluded I could help. I've never been one for trusting my hard-earned money to a banker's care and I'd enough hid away at the shop for me to be able to send it off."

"You've sent off the ransom?" Handle asked, sounding as if unwilling to credit the evidence of his ears.

"Why sure," McKie confirmed in a matter of fact tone. "A young friend of mine happened to drop by and, seeing's time was so short, I figured it best not to let there be any more delay in getting it to Peraro. I'll be expecting you to pay me back, with maybe a little bit of interest, though."

"*Inter*—Oh yes, of course, I'll be delighted to pay it," Handle replied. "But, if there are scouts watching between the border and Escopeta, will your young friend be able to reach Peraro with the money?"

"All he'll need to do is tell them he's got it and they'll *take* him there," McKie replied. "Which being, Mr. Handle, you'll have your niece back safe and sound with you afore sundown tomorrow."

"*Senor Alcalde,* you must come and help me. My wife has beaten me and driven me from my home!"

Startled by the knocking upon the door he had just closed, as he had neither seen nor heard anybody near by as he was returning to his living quarters, Marcos "*el Cerdo*" Bordillo listened to the whining voice which followed the knocking while turning around. The tone and accent was that of a poor *peon,* a number of whom were compelled to live in Escopeta performing such tasks as the *bandidos* considered beneath their dignity, addressing a person of considerable importance.

Annoyance flooded through the *alcalde* as he was distracted from the disturbing train of thought in which he had become engrossed and which had led him to come home alone from *Bernardo's Cantina* so he could devote his full attention to considering its cause. He had never taken, nor performed, his civic duties seriously. Nor, having other things on his mind, was he in any mood to do so at that moment.

One of the factors which had allowed Bordillo to survive,

despite his far from savory attitude towards life, was the possession of considerable low cunning and perception. Added together, they caused him to be far more susceptible to atmosphere than people who made his acquaintance suspected. Employing the latter quality to its full potential, he had become increasingly aware as the evening had gone by that something was troubling each of the men with whom he had been keeping company at the *cantina*.

Enjoyable as it had been to watch, the fight between Florencia Cazador and the kidnapped *gringo* girl had failed to improve the situation. In fact, the *alcalde* had considered there had been a marked deterioration in the relationship between his companions when it ended. He had found the state of affairs puzzling and disconcerting. It was hardly surprising that, being known as her sponsor, Edmundo *"Culebra"* Perez should have been disenchanted and disgruntled by the result. However, Jesus *"Obispo"* Sanchez had appeared much less delighted by the defeat of the Mexican girl than Bordillo—aware of the intense rivalry between the two sub-leaders—had anticipated would be the case.

Mainly though, the *alcalde* had considered it was the attitude of Don Ramon Manuel José Peraro which had been the cause of his misgivings!

From all appearances, the *bandido* chief had been ill at ease even before seeing his mistress lose the fight; which he had authorized against his usual insistence upon good treatment being accorded to kidnap victims until it became obvious no ransom was forthcoming. All the time he had been standing at the bar, prior to learning of the conflict in the "guestroom", he had looked at the front door whenever it opened to admit a new arrival. He had continued to do so while the fight was in progress and throughout the game of Spanish *monte* that had taken place after the combatants were removed. When questioned about this by *Obispo*, he had claimed he was expecting the ransom money to be delivered. Remembering he had never displayed any such interest on the numerous previous occasions when a similar event was forthcoming, Bordillo had been curious about his present preoccupation.

El Cerdo had cared little for the speculations aroused by the untypical behavior of the *bandido* leader!

Normally, knowing himself to be safe under the protective cover supplied of necessity by his family, Bordillo would have cared little for the moods of Peraro and not at all for those of either sub-leader.

On this occasion, having sensed the undercurrents of tension assailing all three, *el Cerdo* had grown increasingly perturbed!

Knowing that Peraro had failed to take the slightest punitive action over the abortive attempts to kill the Ysabel Kid in defiance of his orders to the contrary, the *alcalde* wondered if he was losing his grip. It was not a prospect to be regarded with equanimity by Bordillo. Only the firm hand and personality of Peraro held together the gang and retained the power which made it feared throughout most of Northern Mexico. Should he be deposed by either sub-leader, unless the other was removed at the same time, there would be such dissension that the band would split up. What was more, even if Sanchez or Perez succeeded in their aims, there would be so many desertions by members of the losing factions that those who remained would be severely reduced in numbers. With the gang so weakened, it could not hope to survive.

In such an eventuality, the sanctuary *el Cerdo* found in Escopeta was almost certain to be brought to an end!

Contemplating even an inconclusive and unproven supposition that he might be forced to face the consequences of his past indiscretions, Bordillo was far from enamoured of the interruption to his thoughts. The last thing he wanted at that moment, having gone so far as to eschew feminine company so as to devote his entire attention to the matter, was to have the unimportant problems of a *peon* inflicted upon him.

"*Vamos, hijo de puta!*" *el Cerdo* bellowed, glancing at the quirt hanging on a hook attached to the door. "How dare you come here at this hour to disturb your *alcalde* with such a small thing?"

"She is not a small thing, honored *senor,*" objected the

complainant querulously, showing no resentment at having been described as the 'son of a whore'. "She is very big and fat. Also she hits me with a broom!"

Letting out a furiously profane exclamation which was aroused as much by his anxieties as at the insistence of the whining peasant, Bordillo snatched the quirt from its hook. In the past, he had on more than one occasion delivered summary punishment to a *peon* and was satisfied that he could do so again without danger to himself. Being aware of his exalted status in the community, the caller would not dare to physically oppose the thrashing he intended to administer.

Admission to the living quarters was through a side entrance, which offered greater privacy than via the office portion of the building. Jerking open the door, the *alcalde* was advancing menacingly into the alley when he realized something was not as it should be. There was no sign of the cause of his wrath in the light from the doorway. Even as he was wondering where the speaker might be, the question was answered.

Not, however, in a satisfactory fashion!

Thrusting from the darkness at the left side of the doorway, a hand in a black clad sleeve grasped the front of Bordillo's jacket and gave a jerking swing. Aided by the impulsion of his advance, this propelled him across the alley until he was brought to a halt by colliding against the wall of the adjacent building. Before he could recover either his wits or the breath jolted from him by the impact, he found himself gripped once more and turned to be thrust backwards against the unyielding adobe wall.

"You've got a throat just meant for cutting, *senior alcalde!*" warned a voice. Although it was speaking colloquial Spanish, it was no longer the whining of a *peon*. Rather it was low, hard and savage. The threat it implied was enhanced by something Bordillo suspected was the *very* sharp blade of a large knife touching the skin of his neck. "And, if you make the smallest sound or hesitate before doing *anything* I tell you, I'm going to slice it so deep your head will be hanging down your back."

Always an arrant coward, unless dealing with somebody whose humble status in life made them suitable for bullying, Bordillo felt such terror assailing him that he nearly collapsed. Only the belief that to do so would cause the horrific threat to be carried out gave him the will to remain erect upon legs which felt almost too limp to bear his weight. Perspiration flowed freely down his porcine features and he stood without so much as trying to turn his eyes in an attempt to discover the identity of his captor.

"Wh—What d—do you wa—want?" *el Cerdo* managed to croak after a couple of seconds.

"You!" the voice answered. "I'm taking you with me, *senor alcalde*, to find out whether Don Ramon Peraro will pay my price to get you back. Do *you* think he will?"

"Y—Yes!" Bordillo asserted, having no doubts on the matter.

"Bueno!" the still unseen speaker declared, without removing the knife. "Let's go and collect the horses."

"Wh—Where from?" *el Cerdo* asked.

"From Don Ramon's stable," the voice replied and ended the hope of his captive almost before it came into being. "I know about the guard there and you'd better pray he opens up for you. Because, if he doesn't, or you try to raise the alarm, the mission bells will toll requiem—But you, *senor alcalde*, will be too dead to hear them. You have the promise of *el Cabrito* for *that!*"

CHAPTER FIFTEEN

You'll be the *Second* One I Kill

"Ruiz, it's me. Open up. I want to talk to you!"

"Well, if I won't be 'ternally damned, like most folks say I *will*," breathed the Ysabel Kid, recognizing the voice of the latest arrival at the stable as that of Edmundo *"Culebra"* Perez. *"Gracias, Ka-Dih.* You're surely doing everything you can to help lil ole me!"

Despite what Jock McKie had told Philo Handle in Wet Slim earlier that evening, the young Texan was not carrying the ransom money with which to bring about the release of Mavis Dearington. While walking from the River Queen Saloon, they had agreed that the insistence upon making the rescue bid could have arisen from the disinclination of a hard-headed New England businessman to admit publicly he was unable to produce the sum demanded in the time that had been allowed. Furthermore, as this was of a much shorter duration than was usually the case, they had also considered the possiblity that Don Ramon Manuel José Peraro might have reduced the period in order to offer an excuse for the girl to be sacrificed as a warning to the families of subsequent victims.

While aware that a prompt payment would remove the danger to Mavis, in view of their suppositions, the Kid and the elderly leatherworker had known this would not be forthcoming from her uncle. Nor had the Scot the means at hand by which to achieve her salvation. Being of a generous nature, a trait far from uncommon amongst members of his race — regardless of numerous "ethnic" jokes suggesting the contrary — he had had nowhere near ten thousand dollars in his possession. In spite of feeling confident he could raise the sum the following day, even more quickly than Handle, by sending to the larger bank at the county seat, their conclusions had led them to decide the only hope for Mavis was to induce the *bandido* chief to increase the time at which the payment must be made.

The suggestion of how such a change of mind could be produced had come from the young Texan!

A few years earlier, the Kid had decided against trying to steal the well guarded sire of Peraro's present highly prized stallion as a means of causing trouble between the *bandido* chief and the leader of a rival gang. Despite having created the discord he required,[1] his unbringing as a *Pehnane* Comanche warrior had never allowed him to forget he had rejected such a challenge to his skill as a "raider". Mere pride alone had not been responsible for him contemplating carrying out the theft, so as to use the purloined horse as a "trade" to gain the extra time needed by McKie. He had believed conditions were far more in his favor than on the previous occasion. Then, being away from Escopeta and in the presence of another band of outlaws, the guard would have been much more vigilant than was likely to be the case in the apparent safety of the center of the town which the *bandidos* owned.

Alert to the probability of Peraro having the secret crossing watched, in addition to the other locations at which easy access to Mexico might be obtained, the Kid had not made use of any of them. Instead, he had swum over with his horses at a point which he had felt sure would not be kept under surveillance. On reaching the southern bank of the Rio Grande, he had donned his all black clothing. However having so little time at his disposal, he had not waited to wash the black dye from his big white stallion. Setting off as soon as he was dressed, he had ridden towards Escopeta with all possible speed while still retaining a reserve of energy in each horse to be employed should there be an emergency.

Leaving the three animals in the cottonwood grove which

1. *Told in:* THE BLOODY BORDER. *J. T. E.*

had served a similar purpose on his last visit, the young Texan had entered the town on foot. Making his way towards the stable, he had decided to make an alteration to his plan on seeing Marcos *"el Cerdo"* Bordillo walking alone along the street. Knowing something of the state of affairs between the fat man and Peraro, he had considered something more positive might be effected than merely containing an extension of the period for delivering the ransom.

Capturing Bordillo had proved easy!

Nor had gaining access to the stable been any more difficult for the Kid!

Proving to be as cowardly as was envisaged by his captor, *el Cerdo* had done all he was instructed. On being called by him, the man on guard had not even asked why he was there before unlocking and opening the door of the stable. Using the quirt which had served him so well earlier that evening and which had been tucked into his gunbelt while he was terrifying the *alcalde* into compliance, the Kid had struck down the unwary *bandido* before his own presence could be discovered and resistance offered or an alarm raised. What was more, the silencing was carried out with such speed Bordillo would have been granted no opportunity to shout for help even if he had had the courage to do so.

Still obeying without hesitation, *el Cerdo* had dragged the unconscious guard away as he was told. Then, while his captor bound and gagged the *bandido*, he had set about saddling one of the horses in the stalls. Having completed his task, the Kid had employed one part of his Comanche education to gain the confidence and control of the magnificent black stallion which had been his primary objective. With this achieved, he had been on the point of completing his preparations for departure when a knock on the door had heralded the arrival of Perez.

"Sit down!" the young Texan hissed at Bordillo, extracting the quirt from under his gunbelt with his left hand and drawing the old Colt Dragoon revolver with the right. "Try to warn *Culebra* and you'll be the *second* one I kill!"

Having no doubt that *el Cabrito* could and would do as he had said, *el Cerdo* crumpled into a huddled sitting posture immediately. Although his captor turned and crossed the stable without so much as a backwards glance, he had no intention of trying to warn the man outside. He knew that to do so could allow Perez to take offensive action, or summon assistance which might bring about the death of the black dressed young *Tejano*, but he felt equally certain he would be killed before this could happen. Therefore, having no desire to die, he remained silent and hoped *Culebra* would be able to turn the tables on his captor.

Arriving at the door and ensuring he remained concealed behind it, the Kid drew it open. As had been the case with the guard, the newcomer was far less alert than he would have been under different circumstances. What was more, it seemed he believed there was need for him to enter without delay.

"You took your god-damned time!" Perez snarled, striding rapidly across the threshold. "There's somebody coming and I don't want to be seen coming in he—!"

The words ended as *Culebra* saw enough in the light of the lamp, which was always kept illuminated at night, to realize something was *very* wrong. Even as his gaze swung from the bound and gagged man he had come to see to the cowering *alcalde*, who should not have been present and whose demeanor implied all was far from well, his appreciation of the possibility of danger came too late.

Listening to the drumming of rapidly approaching hooves, the Kid did not waste any time on wondering who might be coming in such haste. Instead, thrusting the door closed with his left foot, he swung the quirt with deft precision. Caught on top of his bare head with the lead loaded butt of the handle, Perez went limp. The hand which had started to reach for his revolver slipped away without touching the butt and he dropped like a steer struck down by a pole-axe.

"Looks like you'd better get to saddling up another horse, *senor alcalde*," the young Texan remarked, tucking the quirt beneath his gunbelt once more. Retaining the Dragoon in his hand while drawing open the door a trifle and watching two *bandidos* on lathered horses go by, he holstered it when he was sure they did not mean to visit the stable. Starting to drag his latest victim towards the stalls by the feet, he went on, "If this keeps on, damned if I won't wind up with half of Don Ramon's boys to trade for that gal he kidnapped."

Having uttered the sentiment, leaving Bordillo to carry out his demand that another mount be made ready, the Kid used his clasp-knife to cut more pieces from the rawhide *riata* he had found hanging on one of the stalls. Using them, he tied Perez far more securely than he had fastened the guard and affixed an equally effective gag. Satisfied he had *Culebra* rendered innocuous, he produced the notebook and pencil he had used when sending the previous message to the *bandido* chief. Writing down what he had done and wanted, he checked the horses were ready for use. Then, helped by *el Cerdo*, he placed and lashed Perez across one of the saddles.

"Get some water and wake that *hombre* up," the Texan commanded, indicating the guard who was already showing signs of regaining consciousness. "Time he's got loose and taken my message to Don Ramon, we'll be long gone. Only you'd best pray to every saint you know that what I say gets done and nobody except Peraro and the *gringo* gal come after us."

"All right, *Cabrito*, I've done as you asked. How do we make the exchange?"

When Ramon Peraro had received the news of what had happened at the stable and what was expected of him, he had already been in a far from amiable mood!

Contrary to the suppositions of the Ysabel Kid and Jock McKie, the *bandido* chief had not had posted lookouts at the various crossing along the Rio Grande. Instead, he had relied solely upon the two men whose arrival had inadvertantly played its part in causing Perez to be captured. They had been in Wet Slim and returned with the news that the rescue bid anticipated by Peraro would not be taking place. Much to their surprise, he had seemed more annoyed than pleased by their information. Dismissing them, he had not returned to bed and was still brooding upon his thwarted plans when the guard from the stable had brought the ultimatum from the young Texan.

On reading the note, the *bandido* chief had known there was another course open and he must do exactly as he was instructed. Even if he was willing to accept the loss of his prize stallion, which he had been warned would be shot at the first suggestion of pursuit, he could not dispense with the respective services of either Perez or Bordillo. Therefore, he had no choice in the matter and, galling as the prospect might be, had to comply or suffer the consequences. The only slight consolation he could draw was that, having been drugged with laudanum to silence her wailing and whining, Florencia Cazador was unconscious. However, being of a more stoic nature, the *gringo* girl had not received similar treatment. Instead, she had been allowed to take a bath and, having received clothing to replace that destroyed in the fight, was now sleeping in the "guestroom."

Sending the guard off to saddle two horses, Peraro had dressed. Then, going next door, he had woken up Mavis Dearington. Giving her a man's shirt, trousers and a pair of moccasins, he had told her to put them on. Taking her to the stable when this was done, he had used his knife to ensure the *bandido* would not spread the word in his absence of the humiliation he was suffering. Leaving the man dead on the floor, he had set off with the girl towards the stripulated rendezvous. While passing through the silent and clearly sleeping town, realizing that *el Cabrito* had entered on two occasions—the second time leaving accompanied by his highly prized stallion and a pair of men—also without being challenged, he had promised himself there would be a tightening up of his security arrangements when he returned.

As was required in the written instructions, full daylight had arrived before the *bandido* chief had seen a black clad figure he recognized walk with empty hands from among the trees some seventy-five yards ahead. Studying the surrounding terrain as he was bringing his horse to a halt, he was willing to concede he would have sought for just such a location if he had been conducting a similar transaction from the side which was making the demands. He and the girl had been riding towards the fairly dense woodland which fringed that section of the Rio Grande, making for the secret crossing as instructed, but there was only completely open ground for more than two miles to their rear. It would have ben impossible, particularly when in contention against a person of *el Cabrito's* proven ability, for anybody—even a single man—to have followed them at a distance sufficiently close to be of use, without being detected.

"Get down from your horses where you are," the Kid called back, also stopping and keeping his hands clear of his sides. "Hang your gunbelt over the saddle and bring the girl forward on foot. I'll shed my rig the same way, then fetch Perez and Bordillo over to meet you. Is that all right with you?"

"What about my stallion?" the *bandido* chief demanded.

"I'll leave him with your other horses, tied to the bushes up here. When me and the girl've ridden off, you can come to collect them."

"How do I know I can trust you to leave him?"

"You've got my word on it," the Kid replied. "Anyways, that old Blackie horse of mine and him likely wouldn't get on too well together should I take him with me. Do we trade my way?"

"I will do as you ask," Peraro affirmed.

Swinging from his saddle and telling the girl to do the same, the *bandido* chief ensured his hands remained in plain view of the Texan while he was removing and draping his gunbelt across its seat. He had agreed to leave the weapons because, having suspected this would be demanded, he had taken a precaution against such an eventuality. He was carrying a second fighting knife in a sheath behind his back, tucked into the waistband of his trousers and with its hilt concealed beneath his waist length *bolero* jacket.

While Peraro was doing as ordered, he heard a whistle and saw the big "skewbald" stallion coming from the woodland followed by his two men. For a moment, he thought it was not the horse usually ridden by the Kid. Then, remembering the reference to "Blackie," concluded it had been disguised. Having an idea why such a precaution had been taken, he glanced at Perez and Bordillo. Both had their arms bound, with their hands obviously tied behind their backs. However, his main attention was directed towards their captor.

What he saw filled the *bandido* chief with a sense of satisfaction!

Unbuckling the black gunbelt, using his right hand only and holding aside the left with the palm upwards, the Kid hung it over the saddle of his horse. Having done so, he gave the order for his captives to start walking. Making what was clearly another sign of good faith, he gave a signal which caused the stallion to stand still as he followed them.

"Come along, *senorita,*" Peraro said, considering everything was going as he required.

Wondering why her uncle was using a stranger to effect her release in such a fashion, Mavis advanced with the *bandido* chief. Despite the grueling experiences of her past twenty-four or more hours, apart from her left eye being swollen and discolored, she gave no sign of what had happened in the barroom of Bernardo's *Cantina*. Such was her superb physical condition, she had thrown off the exhaustion caused by the fight. Apart from a few aches, she was feeling no after effects whatsoever.

"That's close enough," the Kid stated, as the two parties were some fifteen feet apart and they all came to a stop. Stepping between his captives, he stared at the girl for a moment and went on, "Those boys of yours were a mite heavy handed on the lady, Don Ramon."

"Not my men, *Cabrito,*" the *bandido* chief corrected. "Florencia Cazador, you probably don't know her but she's my current mistress, tried to rob Miss Dearington and bit off more than she could chew."

"They had a fight?" the Texan growled.

"The best I've ever seen," Peraro declared. "I must admit the young lady surprised me, the way she went at it."

"You mean you *let* it happen?" the Kid challenged, being aware of how the *bandido* chief was noted for insisting that his kidnap victims received good treatment until it was obvious no ransom was forthcoming.

"Of course," Peraro confirmed. "It was quite an enjoyable sight."

Puzzled by the news he was receiving and not caring for the speculations which it was arousing, the Kid was less alert than would otherwise have been the case. While the conversation was taking place, he had failed to notice Perez was moving back until standing alongside him. Twisting around as his leader was making the admission, *Culebra* sprang into the air. Having his hands bound behind his back did not prevent him from launching an effective attack. Opening his legs, he clamped them around the arms and torso of the young Texan.

Taken completely unawares, the Kid lost his balance and toppled backwards with the black Stetson slipping off as he went down. Its loss proved beneficial. Pinioned by limbs to which much horse riding had given great strength, he was unable to use his hands as an aid to breaking the fall. Fortunately, instead of being driven against the hard ground, the back of his head struck the crown of the hat and it acted as a cushion. However, although he avoided being stunned, he was still far from out of danger or free from trouble. Despite descending upon the left leg of his assailant in what must have been a painful manner, neither this nor having been brought down with him caused the scissor hold to be broken.

"*Pronto, jefe!*" Perez bellowed somewhat breathlessly, the gag having been removed earlier that morning so he could slake his thirst. He knew his leader well enough to feel sure another weapon was available despite the removal of the gunbelt. "I've got the bastard!"

While Peraro had the means of justifying the suppositions of *Culebra,* it had not been his intention to use the knife until *el Cabrito* had turned and was walking away from him. When this had happened, he had meant to draw and throw it. However, seeing the opportunity with which he was being presented, he was all too willing to revise his plan. Watching Bordillo glance back then swing around so as to attack the trapped Texan, the *bandido* chief reached behind him. Passing beneath the bottom of the *bolero* jacket, his right hand grasped the hilt and slid the knife from its sheath.

CHAPTER SIXTEEN

You Were Meant To Be *Killed*

"Blackie!"

Realizing he had never been in graver peril, the Ysabel Kid yelled the name of his big white stallion. At the same time, he was trying to free himself from the grip of the legs Edmundo "Culebra" Perez had wrapped about him. They held firm and he could sense Marcos *"el Cerdo"* Bordillo approaching. Cowardly though the *alcalde* was, he clearly was satisfied he could launch an attack without danger to himself. Either by kicking or stamping, he would be able to add to the difficulties of the Kid. What was more, bringing a fighting knife into view from behind his back, Don Ramon Manuel José Peraro was striding past Mavis Dearington.

Although the young Texan did not know it, help was already forthcoming!

Even before its name was called, seeing the attack upon its master, Blackie gave a snort of fury and lunged forward. At the sight of it rushing in his direction, its mane bristling and eyes seeming to be rolling in rage, Bordillo forgot about going to the assistance of Perez. Trying to change his advance into a very hurried retreat, he tripped and crashed supine to the ground.

Having heard stories about the savagery of the big white stallion owned by *el Cabrito,* the *bandido* chief was all too aware of the danger it posed to his companions. However, he found he had something much closer at hand to distract him. The problem was of his own making. Despite having been told about and seen at first hand the kind of courage which the American girl was capable of displaying, such was his eagerness to avenge the humiliation placed upon him by the kidnapping of his horse and men, he went past her without so much as a glance. Instantly, she sprang and encircled his arms from behind with her own.

Perez heard and guessed what might be implied by the drumming of rapidly approaching hooves, but he was not granted any opportunity to take action for his own protection. Thrusting forward its neck, the magnificent horse siezed him by the right shoulder with its jaws. Pain and alarm caused his legs to relax their hold. Feeling the Kid starting to roll free, he was unable to prevent the escape. Dragged upwards and flung aside, he landed not far from the *alcalde*. Before he had time to gather his wits, much less prepare to fight back, the white stallion was upon him. Screaming in the awesome fashion of its kind when launching an attack, it reared and the iron shod feet smashed down upon him. Shrieking in terror, Bordillo rolled away from the scene of carnage as swiftly as he could force his gross body to move.

Snarling with rage, Peraro began to spread his arms and jerked himself around. Unable to retain her hold, so furiously did he struggle, Mavis was pitched away from him with such violence she could not control her movements or keep her footing. Sent sprawling on to her hands and knees, she saw him recommence his advance. Glancing around, she discovered that the young Texan had escaped from the clutches of Perez and was already springing to his feet. While there was no longer any danger from the other Mexicans, remembering how he had discarded his weapons before coming forward, she assumed he was unarmed and would be at the mercy of the knife held by the *bandido* chief. With a sensation of despair, she realized that she could not hope to rise and intervene a second time before Peraro reached and dispatched him.

Seeing what was happening to Perez gave an added urgency to Peraro as he resumed the interrupted attack. Except for how it affected him personally, he cared not the slightest for the fate of his subordinate. If the attempt to rescue the *gringo* girl had taken place as he expected, he had arranged that neither *Culebra* nor Jesus *"Obispo"* Sanchez would be alive at the end of it. During the fighting, men he trusted were to have assassinated both in a way which would have led their respective adherents to blame the attackers. As it was, because of the activities of *el Cabrito,* he was being robbed of the buffer between himself and the surviving sub-leader.

Other thoughts flooded into the head of the *bandido* chief. According to his watchers in Wet Slim, the intended rescue had been prevented by a Comanche driving off all the horses of the would-be attackers. Yet no Comanche had carried out such a raid for a number of years.

Unless—!

The black dressed young man towards whom Peraro was advancing had Comanche blood!

For some reason of his own, *Cabrito* had elected to carry out the rescue himself and had removed the means by which the larger force would have done so!

The realization did nothing to improve Peraro's state of mind. Rather, it drove out every remembrance of all he had heard about the capability of the Ysabel Kid. Instead of making a careful approach, watchful and ready to deal with whatever defensive measures might be employed by one who—empty hands nothwithstanding—was famous for his skill at knife fighting, his tactics were closer to those of an enraged bull charging blindly to the attack. Coming into range, he sent forward his weapon in a thrust intended to disembowel the cause of his plans being ruined.

Having made the most of the brief yet urgently needed respite granted by the girl delaying the *bandido* chief, the Kid was ready to defend himself. What was more, despite having risen with his hands empty, he was not unarmed as Mavis and his assailant believed.

Like Perez, the Texan had suspected Peraro would be carrying a concealed weapon and had taken a similar pre-caution. Without having allowed either prisoner to see what he was doing, he had opened and tucked the clasp-knife inside the left sleeve of his shirt before leaving the wood-land. It must be admitted, however, that fortune had con-tinued to favor him in spite of the situation having otherwise turned adverse. In addition to his head having landed harmlessly on the crown of the black Stetson, he had had another piece of luck when *Culebra* jumped him. Despite the weapon being far from secure in its place of concealment, necessitating the removal of his gunbelt with the right hand only, the legs which closed around him had trapped it between his forearm and side. This had prevented it from slipping out as he was knocked to the ground and it was still available for use.

Under such circumstances, the kind of reckless attack being launched by Peraro was most ill advised being directed as it was to a person who had won the man-name *"Cuchilo"*—meaning "the Knife"—among the *Pehnane* Comanche by virtue of his skill at fighting with one. It proved to be the most costly error of Peraro's evil and misspent life.

An outwards swing of the Kid's right arm struck the wrist behind the approaching weapon and deflected it. At the same moment, he shook the clasp-knife from the sleeve in which it had been hidden and it slid point first into his waiting grasp. While he could not duplicate the completely ambidextrous prowess of his *amigo*, Dusty Fog, long hours of training enabled him to wield a knife just as competently with either hand. Nor was his ability reduced by having to rely upon one which was so much smaller than his bowie. Like the latter, the clasp-knife had been a producer of the late and great master cutler, James Black. There was, however, one major difference in the manner of its construction. It had been made from the same superlative steel which was used to forge the legendary weapon of James Bowie. No other metal yet made had such strength, nor could take and keep so sharp a cutting edge.

Peraro had only an instant in which to appreciate just how wrong his tactics were!

Thrust beneath the two right arms, the blade of the Kid's knife sliced through Peraro's shirt just above his trousers and made a gash across his stomach. Pivoting aside while delivering the blow, in the fashion of a *matador* avoiding the charge of a bull, the Texan allowed the impetuous rush of the *bandido* chief to carry him by. Although he gave a cry of pain, he was far from incapacitated by the cut and still retained his hold on his weapon.

Knowing his adversary was still far from finished, the Kid completed his evasive turn. Sent out as if delivering a fencing lunge with a rapier, the spear point of the knife sank into Peraro's back and impaled the kidneys. Just as the hard-case had when assailed in a similar manner with the butt of the quirt, the *bandido* chief collapsed. However, his condition was far from critical. While the hard-case had merely been rendered senseless and would recover, he was dying by the time he landed face down on the ground.

Drawing free his knife as Peraro was going down, the Kid took stock of the situation. In passing, he noticed that his gunbelt had been dislodged from the saddle when Blackie attacked Perez and lay a short distance away. Face white as a sheet and showing revulsion, the girl was starting to rise. She was staring to where, sprawled on his back with arms and legs splayed out, *Culebra* made a gory and gruesome spectacle. The steel shod hooves of the stallion had smashed open the skull like a crushed pumpkin and he must have been killed instantly. Close by, babbling prayers for mercy and forgiveness, Bordillo lay face down. His voice was attracting the attention of the horse and it was about to move in his direction.

"Stay put, Blackie!" the Texan barked and, despite the savagery it had displayed whilst dispatching Perez, the stallion obeyed the command.

"Drop the knife!" called a masculine voice with a New England accent.

Starting to swing around without doing as he was told, the Kid found the sight which met his gaze far from pleasant. Recognizing the three men who were approaching from the direction of the woodland, he was more disturbed than relieved by finding they were in the vicinity. Although Philo Handle was not holding a weapon, Ira Jacobs and Andy Evans were each carrying a Winchester rifle in a position of readiness. The events of the past few minutes had kept him so preoccupied that, aided by the springy grass underfoot allowing them to walk very quietly, the trio had contrived to come much closer without the Texan or his horse detecting them than would otherwise have been the case. They were, in fact, only thirty foot or so away when the command was given.

"You heard the boss, 'breed!" Jacobs supplemented, lining his rifle at the Kid as he and his companions came to a halt. "Drop that toad-sticker *now!*"

"And make sure that god-damned stallion of your'n stands still!" added Evans, from the other side of the New Englander, covering the horse just as quickly. "I'll cut him down if he even looks like coming at us!"

"Stand still, Blackie!" the Texan ordered, as the horse gave a snort, knowing nothing would be achieved by allowing it to launch an attack.

For the second time in under seventy-two hours, the life of the white stallion was in jeopardy. On this occasion, however, the Kid knew the situation was infinitely more hazardous. Evans, being aware of how dangerous it was, would not hesitate to carry out the threat. Nor could the Kid hope to prevent this being done. Unlike the three young *bandidos,* his present adversaries were unaware of his presence and had already taken steps to circumvent any intervention he might attempt. Therefore, despite guessing what they intended to do, he realized the moment for taking offensive action had not yet come.

"Uncle Philo!" Mavis gasped, running towards the Texan. "You've making a *mistake.* This young man has *rescued* me."

"So it would seem," Handle replied, glancing at the three Mexicans. "But that *doesn't* endear him to *me.* You see, my dear, you were meant to be *killed!*"

"I just knowed you'd got something like *that* in mind!" the Kid claimed, tossing the knife so its point stuck in the ground in front of him.

"Is that why you took it upon yourself to go to her rescue?" the New Englander demanded.

"No," the young Texan answered. "Jock McKie and me figured's how you might not have enough money on hand to pay Peraro on time, so I came down to see if I could make him wait until you had. Only I saw another way of prying the lady loose and did just that. It wasn't until I found out what's happened to her that I got to reckoning you didn't aim to have her come back alive."

"What made you think that?" Handle asked, being genuinely interested as he realized other people might be able to draw an equally accurate conclusion with regards to his motives and wanting to decide how he must cover his tracks.

As the Kid had belatedly surmised, the New Englander had never had the slightest intention of paying the ransom for his niece. He had invited her to visit the ranch so she could be killed before attaining the age at which she took control of her fortune and discovered his speculations while acting as trustee. The suggestion of how this might be brought about with the least chance of his guilt being established had come from Evans. On being contacted by the hard-case, Peraro had agreed to accept five thousand dollars for making it appear he had kidnapped the girl and she had met her death as a result of an attempt to rescue her. While the rest of the family might suspect the truth, Handle had been confident there was no way they could *prove* he was other than ill-advised in taking action instead of paying. The shortness of the time he had been allowed for making the payment would serve as an excuse for his having gone to her rescue, ostensibly because this was the only way he could envisage saving her life.

After leaving McKie and the peace officers, satisfied they suspected nothing, the New Englander had discussed the events of the evening with Jacobs and Evans. On considering to which tribe of Indians the stealer of the horses was said to belong, in conjunction with the news that the ransom had been sent to Peraro, Evans had guessed the identity of the "young friend" who was making the delivery. In spite of the clothing being different and the color of the horse outside the leatherworker's shop being wrong, the description of the "baby-faced kid" given by Jacobs had also helped him draw his conclusions. He had stated that, having received the stipulated sum of money in the appointed time and being aware of the Ysabel Kid's influential connections in both countries, Peraro would renege on their arrangements and set the girl free.

Being desirous of avoiding the consequences of his illegal

abstractions from the money left in his trust, which would leave him penniless even if he was not prosecuted and sent to prison, Handle had been determined to do all he could to prevent his niece returning to Texas alive. He felt sure that, if she should do so, she would insist upon going back to Providence, Rhode Island, where having her killed would involve far greater risk. Questioning Evans, who claimed it was unlikely the Kid would set out from Escopeta with her before the following morning, he had evolved a scheme.

Waiting until the early hours of the morning, the New Englander and his two henchmen had left to intercept the returning couple. He had written a note to explain their absence, stating he was going to the ranch to collect jewelry and bonds as security against the loan of the ransom money. To support the claim, they had ridden in the appropriate direction until turning off and making for a crossing which Evans had claimed was known only to the border smugglers and other outlaws. He had suggested the Kid might have used it while going to deliver the ransom and could even decide to come back the same way. Even if this was not the case, he had said they could cut across to the shortest trail between the town and border and make the interception.

Reaching Mexico without having been challenged, Evans had gone ahead of his companions to find out whether Peraro had scouts in the woodland. If so, he had intended to ask whether the Kid had gone by and give a false explanation for the presence of his own party. While searching, he had seen the young Texan and the prisoners. Recognizing Perez, Bordillo, and Peraro's black stallion, he had guessed what was happening. Returning with the information, he had led his employer and Jacobs back on foot. Taking advantage of their quarry being engaged in other matters, they had closed in ready to put an end to Mavis and the Kid.

"Peraro's allus been knowed for treating his prisoners real good and gentle, so long's he figured the money he asked for them'd be coming in," the Kid explained, seeking to gain time in which to find a way to escape from his latest predicament. "Which, when I found out he'd let a fight his woman had started with your niece go on, I got to thinking there's only be one reason he'd've done it. He knew the ransom *wasn't* going to get paid. Which looked to me like you'd slickered all those good ole boys back to Wet Slim to ride for Escopeta so's he'd have him a reason to kill her; not because you didn't have the money on hand to send, like Jock and me figures could be."

"So you didn't work that out until *after* you'd met Peraro?" Handle said, looking relieved. "That makes things better. When you don't come back, everybody will think he double-crossed you."

"So you're going to kill us, huh?" the Kid inquired.

"Of course," Handle confirmed.

"Why?" Mavis gasped, staring with horror at the New Englander.

"Greed and caution, my dear," Handle supplied. "I'm your next of kin and I know you *haven't* made a will. With you dead, nobody will find out how much I've abstracted from your fortune. Get it done, men!"

"I want that half breed bastard!" Jacobs claimed. "It was him's put down Jug and Willy in the alley—!"

"And I made *you* look like the yeller bellied snake you are in Jock McKie's shop," the Kid interrupted, standing apparently at ease yet as tense as a compressed coil spring. "You sure backed water there—'Course, you're some braver now seeing's how I don't have no gun."

"All right, you smart-assed son-of-a-bitch!" Jacobs snarled, lowering the rifle until he held it horizontally before him at arms length. "You acted fast that time, let's see happen you can move fast enough to get to your gun."

"That'd be what a gutless skunk like you'd call giving me a fair shake," the Texan said dryly, without taking his eyes from the burly hard-case. "Only thing being, are *you* dead set on going through with it, Mr. Handle?"

"I am," the New Englander stated.

"You don't aim to change your mind?" the Kid asked.

"I don't see any reason why I should," Handle replied.

"I've got some mighty good and *real* tough *amigos* close by," the Kid bluffed. "Fact being, I was going to meet them in Wet Slim last night. I'd left afore they got there, but

Jock'll've told them what's doing. Could be they're on the way to meet up with me already."

"And now we're supposed to look around, so you'll have a chance to get your gun," Handle suggested. "That's a *very* old tri—!"

Showing the high standard of training it had absorbed, the white stallion had been standing like a statue while the conversation was taking place. However, as the New Englander was speaking, its head swung around and tossed. Ears pricked, it gave a snort and stared towards the woodland. Having heard stories about its abilities, Evans glanced in the same direction. What he saw sent a chill of apprehension through him.

"Back there!" the hard-case called, starting to swing around with the rifle still cradled at his right shoulder.

While Jacobs had shared the belief expressed by Handle that the Kid was trying a bluff, the behavior of Evans was different. It caused both of them to duplicate his actions. Only the New Englander turned all the way. About to do so, Jacobs remembered there was a danger much closer to hand than whatever had caused the reaction from the other hard-case.

The assumption was correct!

While the young Texan did not know who might be coming, he appreciated the chance he had been given. With one of his background and upbringing, to think was to act. He made no attempt, however, to reach the gunbelt. Instead, he bent to snatch up the clasp-knife. As he was doing so, a rifle cracked from the woodland and, struck in the head, Evans was killed instantly. An instant later, a second bullet ended the attempt Handle was making to pull his revolver from its shoulder holster. Despite their removal, the Kid knew he was still far from being safe.

Up and down flashed the Texan's right hand. Opening it, he allowed the clasp-knife to fly through the air towards where Jacobs was already looking back in his direction. Even as the weapon left his hand, his instincts warned it was not going to the target for which it was intended. Although it was unlikely to miss entirely, neither would it be sufficient to ensure his safety. Wasting not a split second, knowing there was no time to lose, he sprang away from the girl and threw himself onwards in a dive with hands outstretched before him.

Justifying the summation of the Kid, the knife spiked into the side of Jacobs' neck. Despite having failed to impale at the center and incapacitate him, it was still painful enough to make him drop the rifle and reach upwards. Jerking out the weapon, he flung it aside. Having done so, snarling in rage, he sent his right hand downwards to draw his Colt. He was fast.

Too fast, in fact, for the Kid to have survived without the diversion!

Landing alongside the gunbelt, the Texan snatched the Dragoon from its holster. Rolling on to his left side and grasping the butt in both hands, he thumb cocked the hammer while taking sight. Just as the hard-case's weapon was clearing leather, he squeezed the trigger. Twisting himself over the moment the bullet left the barrel, he dragged back the hammer once more and, coming to rest on his stomach, braced both elbows on the ground ready to fire again.

There was no need!

Rising to strike Jacobs beneath the chin, the .44 ball ranged onwards to erupt through the top of his skull. Flying off in a spray of shattered bone, brains and blood, his hat flew away. He remained erect for a moment. Then, as Mavis screamed at the hideous sight he presented and fainted, the gun dropped unfired from his grasp and he fell.

Letting out a gasp of relief, the Kid allowed the hammer of the colt to descend. Looking around as he started to rise, he was surprised by what he saw. He had expected to discover his rescuers had been Jock McKie and somebody else from Wet Slim, but found this was not the case.

"Hey there, Kid!" greeted Ranger Jefferson Trade, as he and his uncle walked from the trees each carrying his rifle across the crook of his left arm. "Damned if this isn't the *second* time we've had to drop by and save your fool hide."[1]

---

1. *The first occasion is told in:* THE QUEST FOR BOWIE'S BLADE. *This volume also explains how the clasp-knife came into the possession of the Ysabel Kid. J. T. E.*

"By cracky, Jeff, so it is!" the Kid replied. "And, so far's I'm concerned, you can feel free to do it again 'most any time it's needed!"

"If you'll excuse me for saying so, ma'am," Sergeant Brady Anchor drawled. "*You* sure didn't help us to get on to what your uncle was up to."

"That's for sure," Ranger Jefferson Trade seconded, looking past his kinsman. "If we'd knowed it was *your* money he was living off, we'd've been a whole heap less likely to've believed what he told us about why he was so all-fired set on trying to rescue you instead of paying the ransom."

When Mavis Dearington had recoverted from her faint, she found herself lying in the woodland under the care of the stocky sergeant. So capably had he soothed her by the time the two younger men joined them, she had recovered something of the composure and fortitude which had helped her survive a situation far beyond anything her past life had prepared her to endure. They were leading three horses, each carrying a body wrapped in a blanket across its saddle. Announcing they had sent Bordillo back to Escopeta with Peraro and Perez, the rescuer she now knew was called "the Ysabel Kid" had asked if she felt up to going home. On hearing she did, the party had set off. There had been little conversation until they were once more in Texas. Then, noticing how the girl was showing signs of growing strain and repeatedly darting glances over her shoulder at the bodies of the men who had conspired to cause her death, Brady had decided to try and divert her attention. Guessing what his uncle had in mind, Jefferson Trade had offered his support. Nor was the black dressed young Texan slow in lending a hand.

"I'll float my stick along of Brady 'n' Jeff on that," the Kid asserted. "When I asked Jock McKie if he reckoned your uncle was figuring on getting you killed by pretending to be trying to rescue you, I got told's how, you being his poor kin, it didn't seem real likely. So he concluded he maybe couldn't raise the money quick enough to pay Peraro.

Only, being a real proud New England businessman, he was too all-fired to go admitting it to ordinary Texas folks."

"It was Uncle Philo's idea that I should pretend I was dependant upon him," Mavis explained, giving a shudder as she mentioned the name despite feeling better now she had been given something to occupy her mind. "He told me the night I arrived that it would have an adverse effect upon his business prospects if it became known *he* was dependant upon me, so I went along with him."

"I'm not complaining about it, mind, Brady," the Kid declared, deciding a change of subject might be acceptable to the girl. "But just how come you 'n' Jeff were on hand to bill in like you did?"

"Well now," the stocky sergeant replied. "Mr. Handle was mighty convincing, way he told it about not having the money to hand for the ransom, but being peace officers we've got real suspicious minds. So, particularly when Doc Dalrymple came back cussing a blue streak because, like Abe Minsey, he'd been sent out of town on a wild goose chase, we got to wondering if *maybe* we hadn't been told the truth."

"You mean Uncle Philo arranged to have the doctor and the deputy sheriff sent away?" Mavis asked.

"There's nobody else comes to mind who'd have a reason," Brady answered. "With them gone, even if Jock should get by the watchers put to stop him, there wouldn't be anybody else who'd back him in trying to talk the cowhands out of riding to Escopeta. Anyways, thinking along those lines, we reckoned it wouldn't do no harm for us to keep a watch on your uncle."

"That there 'us' means *me*, ma'am," Jefferson Trade put in, as if making the most important point in the conversation. "Uncle Brady had him a good sleep while *I* was keeping watch."

"Which's known far and wide as, 'rank has its privileges', Miss Dearington," the sergeant announced, sounding just as soberly informative. "Top of which, doing it works out better. Way I snore, there's no danger of young Jeff falling asleep while he's doing the watching."

"That sounds reasonable to me," the girl claimed, knowing what the peace officers were trying to do and feeling a little better.

"And *me*," Brady supported. "Anyways, when we saw your uncle and those two hired guns of his sneaking off, we concluded to drift along after them and find out why."

"It's lucky for us you did!" Mavis stated, then swung a glance filled with contrition in the other direction. "I'm sorry, Kid. I didn't mean—!"

"I know," the black dressed Texan interrupted with a grin. "Which being, I was right pleased to see them myself."

"I owe you my life," the girl declared. "I don't know how I can ever hope to repay you for doing it."

"Well now," the Kid drawled. "Happens you've got thirty dollars to spare—?"

"*Thirty* dollars?" Mavis gasped. "Good heavens. Is that *all* you think I'm worth?"

"Shucks, *that* doesn't come into it at all," the Kid replied. "I wouldn't want paying for what I've done, only by doing it I've lost a bet."

In Conclusion

Those of you who read the episode in THE TEXAN upon which this present narrative is an "expansion" may wonder why certain points, particularly the final confrontation, differ from the events recorded in the earlier work. When we questioned Alvin Dustine "Cap" Fog about the inconsistencies, he explained that the source upon which he based the original work did not have access to all the facts. For instance, the information regarding the capture and holding of Mavis Dearington had not then been made available. Also, because at that time there was some conflict of interests between the United States of America and Mexico, it was considered inadvisable to allow the participation of Sergeant Brady Anchor and Ranger Jefferson Trade to be made public as their action might have been constructed as a breach of international law and used to worsen the situation.

Appendix

Raven Head, only daughter of Chief Long Walker, war leader of the *Pehnane*—"Wasp," "Quick Stinger", or "Raider" Comanches' Dog Soldier lodge and his French Creole *pairaivo*,[1] married an Irish Kentuckian adventurer, Sam Ysabel, but died giving birth to their first child. Baptized "Loncey Dalton Ysabel", the boy was raised after the fashion of the *Nemenuh*.[2] With his father away on the family's combined business of mustanging—catching and breaking wild horses[3]—and smuggling, his education had largely been left in the hands of his maternal grandfather.[4]

From Long Walker, the boy learned all those things a Comanche warrior must know: how to ride the wildest, freshly caught mustang, or make a trained animal subservient to his will when "raiding"—a polite name for stealing horses, the favorite pastime of the *Nemenuh* brave-hearts—to follow the faintest tracks and just as effectively conceal signs of his own passing:[5] to locate hidden enemies, or keep out of sight himself when the need arose: how to move in silence through the thickest cover and on the darkest of nights: to be conversant with the ways of wild creatures and, in some cases, imitate their calls so even other members of their kind might be fooled.[6]

The boy had proved an excellent pupil in all the subjects.

He had inherited his father's Kentuckian skill at shooting a rifle. While he was not *real* fast on the draw—taking slightly over a second to bring out and fire his weapon whereas a top hand could practically halve that time—he performed passably with his Colt 1848 Second Model Dragoon revolver. He had won his *Pehnane* "man-name"

178

"Cuchilo"—Spanish for "Knife"—by his exceptional skill in wielding one. It was claimed by those who were best qualified to know that he could equal the alleged designer when fighting with the massive and special type of blade which bore Colonel James Bowie's name.[7]

Joining his father on smuggling expeditions along the Rio Grande, the boy had become known to the Mexicans of the border country as *"Cabrito"*; a name which, although meaning a young goat, had arisen out of hearing white men referring to him as "the Ysabel Kid" and was spoken *very* respectfully in such a context. Smuggling did not attract mild-mannered pacifists, but even the roughest and toughest of the bloody border's brood had soon come to acknowledge it did not pay to rile up Sam Ysabel's son. The Kid's education and upbringing had not been calculated to develop any over-inflated sense of sanctity of human life, no matter what "ethnic-apologists" of a later generation might try to prove to the contrary. When crossed, he dealt with the situation like any *Pehnane* Dog Soldiers—to which war lodge of savage and efficient warriors he had earned initiation— swiftly and in an effectively deadly manner.

During the War Between The States, the Kid and his father had commenced by riding as scouts for Colonel John Singleton "the Grey Ghost" Mosby.[8] Later, their specialized talents and knowledge had been converted to having them collect and deliver to the authorities of the Confederate States in Texas supplies which were run through the blockade imposed by the United States' Navy into Matamoros, or which had been purchased in other parts of Mexico. It was hard and dangerous work, but never more so than on the two occasions they had become involved with missions undertaken by Belle "the Rebel Spy" Boyd.[9]

Soon after the War ended, Sam Ysabel was murdered. While hunting for the killers, the Kid had met Captain Dustine Edward Marsden "Dusty" Fog and Mark Counter.[10] When the assignment upon which they were engaged was brought to a successful conclusion, learning that the Kid no longer wished to continue either smuggling or mustanging, Dusty had offered him employment on the OD Connected ranch. It had been in the capacity as scout rather than ordinary cowhand that he was required and his talents were frequently of the greatest use when carrying out the specialized duties of the spread's floating outfit.[11]

The acceptance of the employment by the Kid had proved of great benefit all round. General Jackson Baines "Old Devil" Hardin obtained the services of an extremely capable and efficient man.[12] Dusty acquired another loyal friend who was ready to stick to him through any kind of danger. For his part, the Kid was turned from a life of comparatively petty crime—with the ever present danger of his activities developing into serious breaking of the law—and became a most useful member of society. Peace officers and honest citizens might have found cause to be thankful for that. His *Nemenuh* education and outlook would have made him a terrible and murderous outlaw, if he had been driven to a life of crime.

Obtaining his first repeating rifle—a Winchester Model of 1866, known as the "old Yellowboy" because of its brass frame, although at first referred to as the "New Improved Henry"—while in Mexico with Dusty and Mark, the Kid soon became a master in its use. At the first Cochise County Fair in Arizona, he had won the first prize in the rifle shooting competition against stiff opposition.[13]

The prize was one of the magnificent and legendary Winchester Model of 1873 rifles which qualified for the title, "One Of A Thousand"![14]

Among the Kid's other activities, in part, it was through his efforts that the majority of the Comanche bands had agreed to go on to the reservation, following the circumvented attempts to ruin the signing of the peace treaty at Fort Sorrel.[15] Nor could Dusty Fog have cleaned out the outlaw town called "Hell" without his assistance.[16] He had also accompanied Miss Martha "Calamity Jane" Canary when she went to claim a ranch she had inherited, which proved to be as hectic a time as he had ever spent.[17]

---

1. Pairaivo; first, or favorite, wife. As is the case with other Comanche names, this is a phonetic spelling based upon: COMANCHES, Lord

Off The South Plains, *by Ernest Wallace & E. Adamson Hoebel, 1952, University of Oklahoma Press.*

2. *Nemenuh: "the People", the name given by the Comanaches to their nation. Members of other Indian races with whom they came into contact called them, frequently with good cause and ethnic-apologism notwithstanding, Tshaoh, "the Enemy People".*

3. *A description of the methods used by mustanger's is given in :* .44 CALIBER MAN *and* A HORSE CALLED MOGOLLON.

4. *Told in:* COMANCHE.

5. *An indication of how well the Ysabel Kid could conceal tracks and the methods he employed can be found in:* Part One, "The Half Breed", THE HALF BREED *and its preposed "expansion,"* WHITE INDIAN.

6. *An example of this knowledge and ability is given in:* Part Three, the Floating Outfit (The Ysabel Kid), "A Wolf's A Knowing Critter", J. T.'s HUNDREDTH.

7a. *Some researchers claim that the actual designer of the knife was James Bowie's elder brother, Rezin Pleasant. It was made by the master cutler, James Black, of Arkansas. (A few authorities state the manufacturer was Jesse Cliffe, a Caucasian blacksmith employed on the plantation of the Bowie family in Rapides Parish, Louisiana). As all the knives of James Black were hand-made, there were variations in their dimensions. The specimen owned by the Ysabel Kid had a blade eleven and a half inches long, two and a half inches wide and a quarter of an inch thick at the guard.*

7b. *According to William "Bo" Randall of Randall Made Knives, Orlando, Florida—a master cutler and noted authority on the subject—Bowie's knife weighed forty-three ounces, having a blade eleven inches long, two and a quarter inches wide and three-eighths of an inch thick. His Model 12 "Smithsonian" bowie knife is modeled upon it, one of which being in the possession of Mark Counter's great-grandson, James Allenvale "Bunduki" Gunn—the sobriquet being derived from the Swahili word for a hand-held firearm of any kind—for whom we also have the honor to be biographer and whose adventures are recorded in the Bunduki series.*

7c. *One fact all "bowie" knives have in common regardless of their size is a "clip" point, wherein the last few inches of the otherwise unsharpened back of the blade joins and becomes an extension of the main cutting surface in a concave arc. A "spear" point, on the other hand, is formed by the sides coming together in symmetrical curves.*

7d. *What happened to James Bowie's knife after his death during the final assault at the siege of the Alamo Mission, San Antonio de Bexar, Texas, on March the 6th, 1834, is told in:* GET URREA *and* THE QUEST FOR BOWIE'S BLADE.

8. *Colonel John Singleton "the Grey Ghost" Mosby makes a "guest" appearance in:* Part One, The Futility of War", THE FASTEST GUN IN TEXAS *and its "expansion",* A MATTER OF HONOR.

9a. Told in: THE BLOODY BORDER *and* BACK TO THE BLOODY BORDER *(Berkley Books' 1978 U.S.A. edition retitled:* RENEGADE.

9b. Further details of the career and special qualifications of Belle "the Rebel Spy" Boyd are recorded in: THE COLT AND THE SABRE; THE REBEL SPY; THE HOODED RIDERS; THE BAD BUNCH; SET AFOOT; TO ARMS! TO ARMS! IN DIXIE!; THE SOUTH WILL RISE AGAIN; THE QUEST FOR BOWIE'S BLADE; *Part Eight, Belle "the Rebel Spy" Boyd, "Affair Of Honor," J. T. 'S* HUNDREDTH; THE REMITTANCE KID—*which is listed among the titles of the* Calamity Jane *series for convenience, although "Calam" does not appear in it*—THE WHIP AND THE WAR LANCE *and Part Five,* "The Butcher's Fiery End". J. T. 'S LADIES.

10a. Told in: THE YSABEL KID.

10b. Details of the careers of Captain Dustine Edward Marsden "Dusty" Fog and Mark Counter are given in various volumes of the Floating Outfit *series. The former also features prominently in the* Civil War *series.*

11. "Floating Outfit": a group of four to six cowhands employed by a large ranch in the "open range" period to work the more distant sections of the property. Taking food in a chuck wagon, or "greasy sack" on the back of a pack animal, they would be away from the ranch house for long periods and so were the pick of the crew. Because of the prominence of General Jackson Baines "Ole Devil" Hardin in the affairs of Texas, the floating outfit of the OD Connected ranch was frequently sent to assist such of his friends who found themselves in difficulties or endangered.

12. Information regarding the career of General Jackson Baines "Ole Devil" Hardin is given in the Ole Devil Hardin *and* Civil War *series. However, as a result of being confined to a wheelchair by the accident recorded in the* "The Paint" *episode of* THE FASTEST GUN IN TEXAS, *he plays no active part in the* Floating Outfit *series. The General's sobriquet arose during his younger days, out of his habit of emphasising the Mephistophelian aspects of his features and because his contemporaries claimed he was a "lil ole devil for a fight".*

13. Told in: GUN WIZARD.

14. When manufacturing the extremely popular Winchester Model of 1873 rifle, the makers selected those having barrels found to shoot with exceptional accuracy to be fitted with set-triggers and given a special fine finish. Originally the chosen arms were inscribed, "1 of 1,000", but this was later changed to script, "Out Of A Thousand". However, the title was a considerable understatement. Out of a total production of seven hundred and twenty thousand, six hundred and ten rifles, only one hundred and thirty-six qualified for the distinction. Those of a slightly lower quality were given the name, "One Of A Hundred", but only seven were made. The practice was commenced in 1875 and discontinued in 1878, allegedly because the management decided it was not good sales policy to suggest the Company produced different grades of rifles.

15. *Told in:* SIDEWINDER.

16. *Told in:* HELL IN THE PALO DURO *and* GO BACK TO HELL.

17a. *Told in:* WHITE STALLION, RED MARE.

17b. *Details of the career and special qualifications of Miss Martha "Calamity Jane" Canary are given in the various volumes of the* Calamity Jane *series. She also makes "guest" appearances in:* Part One, "The Bounty On Belle Starr's Scalp", TROUBLED RANGE; Part One, "Better Than Calamity": THE WILDCATS; THE BAD BUNCH; THE FORTUNE HUNTERS; Part Two, "A Wife For Dusty Fog", THE SMALL TEXAN; TERROR VALLEY *and* GUNS IN THE NIGHT.

17c. *While the first two titles listed above have been "expanded" under the respective titles,* CALAMITY, MARK AND BELLE *and* CUT ONE, THEY ALL BLEED, *on supplying us with the added material—which in some cases differs form the source we used when working on the original manuscripts in the early 1960's—Andrew Mark "Big Andy" Counter made the proviso they must be included in the* Calamity Jane *and not the* Floating Outfit *series. He did not explain why he wished this to be done, nor did we ask; but we have adhered to his wishes.*